THIEVES IN THE TEMPLE

A JACOB AND MIRIAM MYSTERY

RICHARD FREEBORN

For Jackie

CHAPTER ONE

The Babylonian New Year Festival
Day Five - Morning

It was barely dawn, the sky in the east bright, although the sun was still below the horizon. Despite the early hour, the major streets of the city of Babylon were busy with worshippers and celebrants. The Babylonian crowds pushed and shoved their way west along the wide thoroughfare of Marduk Street toward the Esagila: the massive temple complex dominating the eastern end of Marduk Street, and almost as imposing as the royal palace to the north.

It was the fifth day of the Babylonian New Year Festival, the first day after the priests completed their private rituals with the gods. The first day, the rest of the city's inhabitants could take part in the festivities.

Spring was early that year and the heat of the previous day still radiated from the walls; three or four times a man's height that bordered the street. Decorating the walls, mosaics of wild animals growled and snarled down at the crowds as they fled the representations of Babylonian nobles engaged in hunting them down.

Even with the pushing and shoving, the mood of the crowd was good natured, festive and in a holiday mood. It would be another six or seven days before many of them had to return to the regular toil of their daily work.

On this fifth day of the Babylonian New Year Festival, ritual dictated King Nebuchadnezzar return from the city of Borsippa by barge with the sacred image of the god Nabu, Marduk's son in his possession. The priests and their acolytes had begun the ritual cleansing of Nabu's shrine within the Esagila long before dawn. Although it would be well into the afternoon before the king arrived, the crowd was eager to be there early so they could be inside the Temple precincts and watch the first of the public ceremonies.

While the crowd drifted like the gentle meandering flow of the nearby Euphrates river, one man eased and weaved his way through the throng with a purpose. His long tunic was the same naturally faded white as the sheep who'd given its coat to make the cloth. It contrasted with the colorful dyed linen tunics and woolen over-tunics worn by the revelers who had dressed carefully in their best clothes. The warm morning had encouraged most of them to leave off their traditional short cloak, but none of the men had discarded the carefully wound turbans that covered their heads.

The man's dark face showed no emotion as he stepped to one side, allowing a laughing family to go past, turning to protect his right side, and the bundle he carried in the crook of his right arm. His brown eyes were clear and alert as he watched the father and oldest son pause beside him. The son's dark eyes studied the man, noticing the pointed shape of the man's beard in contrast to their own beards, trimmed square, like the blade of a shovel.

"Ahum," the son said. Foreigner.

One woman in the group heard the boy. She turned and looked back at them, then said something in a sharp tone, the fragrance of her cypress oil perfume hanging in the air. The men shrugged, nodding at the man and rejoining their families.

He watched them for a moment, then resumed his journey, turning north onto Sin Street and then right into the smaller side streets of the Old City. It was quieter here, there were fewer people, and the high walls of the houses reduced the crowd noise to a low buzzing like bees hunting for nectar.

There were no Temples on these streets, but shallow niches carved into the mud-brick house walls held shrines dedicated to the various gods of the Babylonian pantheon. He ignored them, lengthening his stride and making turns into successive streets with the confidence of a man knowing where he was going, and eager to get there.

He made one last right turn onto a street that ended against the imposing height of the Inner City wall. The wall was thirty paces thick and nearly nine-hundred courses of bricks high. The man had been proud of the city walls of his native Jerusalem, but acknowledged the feat of the Babylonians, not only to build walls this tall, but wide enough to drive chariots along.

He paused at the first house on the right where the door was open. An elderly man stood in the doorway, leaning on a cane. His thin wispy beard carried a heavy dusting of gray and silver streaks. As the younger man approached him, the old man straightened, a smile brightening his lined features. He kept his left hand on the cane and reached his right to grip the other man's hand.

"It's good to see you, Jacob. I'll follow you inside."

"And good to see you, Solly," Jacob said, releasing the man's hand and stepping past him into the interior. He was in a small covered hallway with a niche to the right. There was a mud-brick bench built into the wall and a narrow shelf with an unlit clay lamp. Solly's wool cloak lay folded neatly across the bench.

Two more steps and Jacob came out into the extensive enclosed courtyard maybe forty paces long and twenty or more wide. The sandy colored mud-brick walls rose on all sides and the second floor balconies looked down into the still shadowed courtyard where the air remained pleasantly cool.

There were two men, two women, and three children standing together in a loose group. They turned to watch as he approached, and Jacob felt his breath catch as the younger of the two women lifted her head and her brown eyes met his. Miriam, a cousin to Esther, the other woman in the group. The two men were Esther's husband, Isaac, and his brother Amos.

Jacob hadn't expected Miriam to be here. The previous after-noon, a woman in the Outer City had requested Miriam's help while her daughter gave birth. Miriam wasn't a healer or mid-wife by train-ing, but during the desert trek that brought thousands of Judeans into Exile, she'd learned about herbs for aches and illnesses and pregnan-cies. As the widow of a priest, people trusted her.

Seeing Miriam there, the rich black hair falling around her face, and cascading down across her shoulders, Jacob felt the surge of emotion he always felt when he saw her. They were betrothed, although no date was set for their marriage. It was one of several matters he needed to discuss with Isaac.

Miriam.

She was nothing like his wife. Nothing like the girl who'd cursed the marriage their parents had arranged, or the woman who cursed him again as she lay dying when the healers could not stop the bleeding while the shriveled, bloodied body of their still-born son rested on her chest.

Miriam was the first woman Jacob had looked at, or cared about, in the seven years he'd been a widower. Maybe the first woman he'd ever really cared for. The thought disturbed him.

"I'm sorry to be late," he said, coming back to the present, and returning Miriam's smile. "The Festival crowds are the worst I've seen in the four years we've been Exiled from Jerusalem."

The oldest man, Isaac, smiled sympathetically. "A few minutes here or there are of no concern, Jacob. Welcome again to my home and thank you for joining us to say Shema." His voice was deep and rich coming from deep inside his large body. A body that caused his long tunic to strain across the chest and stomach. He nodded toward the other man: slimmer and slightly shorter but clearly his brother. "Amos was out earlier and said you'd have a problem with the crowds. Are we ready?"

Jacob nodded and shook out the woolen ivory-colored prayer shawl nestled in the crook of his right arm. He felt the stab of pain in his right arm as he swung the ivory shawl over his shoulders, the legacy of a wound gained fighting the Babylonians one night on the Mount of Olives. Jacob adjusted the shawl so the white tassels hung free from the blue fringe cord.

Isaac stepped forward and looked Jacob over, checking how the shawl lay on Jacob's shoulders. Nodding approval, Isaac checked his brother, and then the three boys, all less than ten summers old, each of whom fidgeted as their father made necessary adjustments. Satisfied, Isaac nodded and his look became serious as he turned away. Isaac moved to the front of the family group, cleared his throat with a loud cough, and swung his arms out and up until his outstretched fingers pointed toward the sky.

Jacob had seen this flamboyance in Isaac's actions many times. It always seemed wrong to him. It reminded him of the Temple priests in Jerusalem. The men who spoke and preached of righteousness and commitment to the covenant, but lived very different lives.

Something made Jacob look up, and he caught Miriam looking at him. She'd told him about her life as the daughter, and wife of a priest. There was a sad look in her dark eyes that told him she felt the same way about Isaac's celebration of the morning ritual.

Jacob inclined his head slightly toward her and joined the rest of Isaac's family in the first words of Shema, even though the words echoed dry and hollow in his head, and he no longer felt the gift of life and energy the words had once given him: "Praised are you, Lord our Yahweh, King of the universe, creating light and fashioning darkness, ordaining the order of all creation."

CHAPTER TWO

The Babylonian New Year Festival
Day Five - Morning

"Rock of Israel, rise to Israel's defense. Fulfill Your promise to deliver Judah and Israel. Our Redeemer is the Holy One of Israel, Adonai tzeva'ot is His name. Praised are You, Redeemer of the people Israel."

There was a moment of silence, even more intense after Isaac's deep booming voice made the words of the final blessing reverberate from the mud bricks around the courtyard.

The three boys chattered in high-pitched voices and tugged at the shawls on their shoulders, untangling their arms and tossing them toward Esther. They clustered around her, begging in high plaintive voices to be allowed to eat.

Esther gathered the shawls, and with a sigh of acquiescence, gestured at the two Babylonian servants hovering in the kitchen's doorway. The two women came forward carefully, avoiding the children, and carrying yellow-glazed platters of dates, melons, and barley bread.

Jacob let the chatter wash over him, hoping it would fill the empty feeling in his head and heart. Once Shema had been the morning ritual that filled him with energy for the coming day. Now it was a litany of seemingly meaningless words he could recite without thought or contemplation. Was he spending too much time with the Babylonians, and being influenced them, as many other Exiles accused him? He didn't think so, but what other explanation was there for how the ceremony failed to move him anymore? Jacob shook his head, and lifted the shawl from his own shoulders, careful to protect the patches of wear that threatened to tear the shawl into a series of ragged woolen fragments.

When he looked up, Miriam was standing before him, her rich brown eyes studying the garment in his hands.

"That shawl gets more ragged every time I see you wear it, Jacob. The tassels are pulling away, and I can't allow my future husband to look poorly dressed during Shema."

There was a gentle teasing tone to her voice, and despite his mood, Jacob couldn't keep the smile from his face.

"I've had this shawl since before the siege of Jerusalem," he said. "I suppose I should replace it, but it's maybe the last connection I have with our life in Judah and the freedom that went with it. I can't let it go that easily."

"Nor should you," she agreed. "I can repair it, if you'd like. I promise you won't be able to see the mending."

In the fresh morning light flooding into the courtyard, Jacob could see the firm lines of her cheeks and jaw, and the fine lines crinkling the smooth olive skin around her mouth and eyes. It was a face that had seen much, and he knew she'd only told him a small part of it. It was a strong face as well, determined and backed by a strong will.

Jacob suspected she was going to be a handful after they were married, and he welcomed the challenge. He appeared to consider her offer for a moment longer, then handed her the garment.

As Miriam took the shawl, their hands touched, and hidden by the folds of wool, Jacob twisted his palm and squeezed her fingers.

Her eyes darted to one side for a moment as her brown cheeks darkened slightly with a flush, before she realized their hands were hidden from view. She gripped his hand in return, then stepped away, taking the shawl with her.

"I'll keep it somewhere safe and work on it later. It will be ready for you in the morning. Now eat before Isaac spoils your appetite," she said, a sympathetic smile brightening her face.

"He's worried," Jacob replied with a smile of his own, appreciating her concern. "I expect it's the trading caravan to Jerusalem. It's one of the largest he's ever attempted and every step we move forward there's another block or impediment. It takes time, but I believe we'll get everything resolved."

"I hope so, because then he might allow us to set a date."

She turned away, and Jacob watched the cascade of black hair swing across both sides of her back as she walked toward the doorway into the living quarters of the house.

When she disappeared inside, Jacob turned his attention to the breakfast platters and selected a flat slice of barley bread, added dates and a piece of melon carved in the arc of a new moon. He placed a date in his mouth, letting the sweet, gritty flavor explode in his mouth. It wasn't the grapes and olives he preferred and had grown up with in Jerusalem, but it was sustenance.

"I'm trying to think of a way to store olives so we can bring them back from Jerusalem," Isaac said, coming up beside Jacob.

Isaac reached out his hand, and his short, stubby fingers selected a handful of dates. He squeezed one between his fingers until juices began oozing from the slit where the stone had been removed.

"Olive oil would be good as well," Jacob agreed. "I can't get used to the taste of the sesame oil the Babylonians use for cooking. It changes the flavor of anything you cook, vegetables or meat."

"I don't know there's a profit in bringing olive oil from Judah, but a few jars for our own use wouldn't go amiss," Isaac agreed, pushing another date into his mouth, and talking as he chewed. "What's this I hear about another delay? The caravan was supposed to leave before the start of the New Year Festival. Is your caravan master, Eli not ready?"

"Readier than all of us," Jacob said. "Unfortunately, like us, he's Judean and we need special permission for him to leave the city and travel to Judah. I'm working to have Arioch give his permission, but he's one of the senior priests at the Temple of Marduk and has substantial responsibilities during the New Year Festival. He's a little distracted at the moment."

"A curse on Nidintu," Isaac said in a level voice. "His little escapade of revenge against Bel Ibni has put us all at risk. Do you have any idea what it's costing us to store the linens and other goods we have ready?"

Jacob nodded slowly as he chewed a piece of the melon. He had a substantial part of his own wealth linked to the caravan. He knew the storage costs to the last piece of silver, and every delay put him at more risk than either Isaac or Bel Ibni.

"I'm as frustrated as you are, Isaac. I should have known Nidintu was Bel Ibni's cousin. Since Nidintu left the city, Bel Ibni considers the whole barley crop affair to be my fault."

"You need to talk some sense into Bel Ibni, Jacob. If he's still making business decisions based on the advice of a mistress with a pretty face, like he did with that barley crop, we need to cut our ties before he drags us all down."

"At the moment, I don't know where I stand. Bel Ibni is arranging caravans I'm not told of, and most of my conversation with him is through his son, Horam."

"At least the boy has some sense," Isaac said. "Caravans to where?"

"Harran, if my sources are correct. I asked Horam about it, but he claimed to know nothing."

"Probably doesn't," Isaac shook his head and helped himself to another handful of dates, scowling as his boys shrieked in excitement at something Esther had said to them. "I'm disappointed with Arioch. After the times you've helped him and saved his position in the Temple, I expected more cooperation and gratitude."

"Arioch is a priest, Isaac. I never had much cooperation or gratitude from the ones in Solomon's Temple. Arioch has to deal with factions who oppose every step our people take to becoming accepted in Babylon. Many of them want us to be slaves like we were under the Pharaohs in Egypt."

Isaac sighed, picked up a piece of barley bread, inspected it while sucking his lips in and out. He frowned and replaced the bread onto the platter. "I know, but I'd rather he helped more directly."

Jacob nodded in a way he hoped signified agreement without actually having to say anything. He knew better than Isaac the challenges Arioch faced from the many factions inside the Temple of Marduk.

He returned the conversation to Bel Ibni. "Getting Bel Ibni's attention during the New Year Festival will be nearly as difficult as getting Arioch's but I'll do what I can."

"Good. And one more thing. Are you sure the Judah caravan is the right place for my brother?"

Jacob glanced across the courtyard to where Amos was eagerly attacking a plate piled with bread and dates.

"Amos isn't as soft as you think, Isaac. Becoming involved with the caravan has given him a purpose again. As a Judean, he'll be accepted more readily in Jerusalem than any Babylonian will be. I've also told Eli and his wife more than once to keep Amos away from the wine and those Armenian spirits he's fond of. I'll remind them at least one more time before the caravan leaves."

Isaac nodded, and reached for another piece of melon, his pudgy hand pausing and hovering at Jacob's next words. "I want to set a date for my wedding to Miriam."

Isaac's hand paused a moment longer, then descended and snared two pieces of melon. "Not now. After the Judah caravan," he said. "We'll talk about it after the caravan returns," and he turned away toward his children, leaving Jacob standing alone, and with nothing to do other than leave.

CHAPTER THREE

The Babylonian New Year Festival
Day Five - Morning

The floor of palm logs sagged and bounced as Miriam stepped out of her room and onto the balcony that ran round the upper story of Isaac's home, just high enough to catch the soft breeze that came over the high city walls to her left. The logs moved every time she stepped out onto them, which was at least once a day, and the slight shudder under her feet always made her heart beat a little faster.

Miriam knew her reaction made no sense. Nothing had happened in the three years she'd been living under Isaac's roof, and he was too careful a man to let harm befall his family through negligence.

She still had Jacob's shawl draped over her right arm and put her left hand on the smooth rail of palm wood to steady herself. The balcony was still in shadow, and she could watch the conversation between Isaac and Jacob below her without being seen.

The men stood close together as they picked at the bread and dates on the table before them. Miriam was too far away to hear what they said, but from the way they stood, she could tell it was an awkward conversation.

Miriam could also tell from the way Jacob frowned and turned away, the end of the conversation had not been to his liking. He hid it well though, smiling and exchanging words with Solly. Words that made both men laugh as Jacob went into the narrow hallway leading to the street.

She'd known Jacob for just over a year now. No, closer to two years, and she shook her head at how the time had gone by. The first time she and Jacob met had been at the celebration of Isaac's business partnership with Bel Ibni. Jacob had been an adversary that day when he thought her to be a thief. Applying even a loose interpretation of the commandment, he was right. Miriam had admitted she stole the lucky stones Bel Ibni proudly displayed in his business room.

Jacob had no reason to believe her when she told him the stones were the Urrim and Thummin from the Temple of Gath; holy artifacts used by the priests for divining Yahweh's will and looted during the Babylonian invasion.

Even then she'd felt an attraction to him, tried to deny it and keep him at a distance. It hadn't worked that way, especially when he had copies of the stones made and delivered them back to Bel Ibni. The originals were given to Ezra, the closest the Exiles had to a high priest.

Jacob had an energy and vitality that her first husband lacked. Not surprising, she thought, Jacob was still fifteen years younger than the priest her father had insisted she marry. A marriage that took place weeks after her first blood coursed and she became a woman.

There was a scuffle and scraping from the room behind Miriam. It was an arrival she'd been expecting, and she turned toward the doorway as her cousin Esther came out of the sleeping room. Esther had one pudgy hand on her chest and leaned the other on the balcony railing as she paused and huffed a cough that turned her plump cheeks a rich scarlet.

Esther had been pregnant with her fourth child when the Babylonians conquered Jerusalem. She had lost the baby in the second week of the journey into Exile and nearly died.

While she recovered, Esther still had to manage three young boys and the trek across the desert. Miriam had joined the family part way through that time. Her husband, the priest, had walked away from their camp one evening and disappeared. He wasn't the first, or the last to end their journey into Exile that way.

Instead of sorrow, Miriam had felt only relief.

Gray streaks threaded through Esther's dark hair. Lines furrowed her forehead and down around a mouth set in a thin line of disapproval. She held the railing loosely for support and breathed deeply. She looked fourteen years older than Miriam instead of four.

"Are you all right?"

"I will be," Esther wheezed, her chest heaving as she breathed deeply a few more times and put more weight on the railing so it creaked in protest. "I came to see if you need help with that shawl. From what I could see of it, I suspect there will be more to these repairs than simply replacing the cord and reattaching the fringes."

Miriam thought so, too.

"Let's find out." Carefully Miriam unfolded the ivory colored garment, letting the soft wool lie across her forearms. The fringes were even more ragged than she expected. The blue cord at each corner was faded and frayed. Patches of the material where they had rubbed against Jacob's shoulders were almost transparent, and she could clearly see the tan color of her own robe through the thin strands of wool.

Esther ran her stubby fingers over the material, clicking her tongue with disapproval. "At least it's excellent quality wool," she said finally. "But it needs a lot of careful, detailed work. Are you sure you're capable of making repairs this extensive, Miriam?"

Miriam turned her head away, looking out over the roof on the other side of the courtyard so Esther wouldn't see the flush of anger she felt burning her cheeks. She took a breath, low and shallow so it didn't show. The way she'd learned so as not to provoke her husband. She kept her voice low and even.

"This is nothing compared to the repairs my father and the other priests of Gath expected. I may not have it completed by the morning, but I will finish the repairs."

"If you say so. I have wool that should match, but you must find some new blue cord. I used the last of it when I made the boys their shawls."

Esther let the material drop from her fingers and shrugged. "I wouldn't spend too much time on it, Miriam. Isaac is concerned Jacob spends too much time with the Babylonians. Give him until the end of the summer and he'll be trimming his beard like a spade and pretending to be one of them. After that your work will be for nothing and Jacob will be up in the Esagila praying to Marduk or whichever of their gods he thinks offers him the most."

"I think you, and Isaac, are misjudging the depth of Jacob's faith."

Esther's head came up and her dark eyes glittered. The desire to show compassion was something else she'd lost in the desert.

"You might have learned something if your husband had lived, Miriam, but you know nothing of how the world works, or how men think. Isaac conceded much to Jacob over your bride price, but there's no talk of a wedding is there. Has Jacob discussed it with you?" Esther paused, and when Miriam didn't answer, her voice was triumphant. "I thought not. What holds him back other than his desire to please that priest at the Esagila? What's his name? Arioch? You listen to me, cousin. Jacob will run errands for those people within two or three moons. There'll be no shame if you tell him now. Tell him there's no future with you."

Under the shawl, Miriam clenched her hand into a tight fist, feeling the nails bite into her palm. The sudden stab of pain calmed her. Miriam had heard Esther one night when she'd had one wine too many. If there wasn't a rich potential husband available with a good bride price, Esther would prefer Miriam stayed in their household as a surrogate mother for the boys, and someone regarded as little more than a favored servant.

Miriam wanted to scream at Esther; tell her how Amos and his drinking and gambling had nearly cost Isaac everything; would have done so if Jacob hadn't intervened and put himself at risk.

Instead, Mirim said nothing. She had given Jacob her word and learned the value of silence before she became a widow. Until Jacob released her from her promise, she would endure Esther's bitterness. It was nothing compared to the lessons she'd learned from her husband.

Miriam took another breath, more pronounced this time, and turned to face her cousin. Once again, she controlled her tone.

"I think the delays with the caravan to Judah have them both on edge, although there seemed no tension when I saw them speaking earlier. My husband, the High Priest of Gath, told me before he died, these were things I didn't need to worry about or try to understand."

Esther scowled, and there was something in her dark eyes. A suspicion that Miriam was being disrespectful, except Esther couldn't decide how.

Miriam kept her face still and emotionless until Esther made a noise of frustration that was almost a growl.

Miriam watched Esther's back as her cousin walked away along the balcony. Esther would never know what, or how much, Miriam had learned before she became a widow.

CHAPTER FOUR

The Babylonian New Year Festival
Day Five - Morning

The sun had risen above the horizon when Jacob left Isaac's house. The light creeping over the city walls and down into the streets of Babylon. The sunlight highlighted the patterns in the ridges on the pale-brown mud-brick walls. It was still too early for the heat to continue the rotting process of the refuse littering the streets, and Jacob could breathe easily without having to cover his face from the stink, as he knew he'd have to do later in the day.

The chatter of the New Year revelers making their way to the Esagila along Marduk Street and Processional Street was a soft background noise like flies buzzing around food left in the open. There were fewer people in the back streets, and Jacob walked quickly and unhindered toward the eastern edge of the Inner City, past the Greek theater, and toward his own home.

As he walked, he felt the knot of frustration in his stomach ease.

The knot wouldn't go away completely until he knew why Isaac was delaying any serious conversation about his marriage to Miriam. Isaac usually had a reason for everything he said or did; measuring each action against a perceived or potential gain.

Usually, Jacob could work out and understand Isaac's motives, but not this time. This time Jacob had no idea what Isaac wanted, or what he was thinking. The situation made no sense to him. Isaac had spent several moons hinting that Miriam would make Jacob a good wife, had even spoken with the prophet Ezra frequently. Isaac had presented a bride price that protected Miriam, but was acceptable to everyone given Jacob's limited wealth.

The agreement was for a nominal sum with a commitment to pay the full bride price if, for any reason, Jacob and Miriam separated or divorced. It was a generous offer, and one Jacob had readily accepted. It added to Jacob's confusion that having met the terms of the bride price, and was now pressing to set a marriage date, Isaac was vague and non-committal.

The shrill chatter of excited children pulled Jacob out of his thoughts and back to the present as a group of families with three boys and two girls came out of a street and toward him from the opposite direction. The children wore robes that had been washed and repaired and had yet to gain marks and stains inflicted by their boisterous and enthusiastic owners.

The youngsters, none of them older than seven or eight years, weaved around their parents, then extended their whirling scampering runs to include Jacob in the pattern before linking hands and dashing forward once more their voices high and excited as they kicked up small spurts of dust with every step. Jacob couldn't help but smile and nod a greeting to the two fathers, one of whom he recognized as a neighbor from his own street.

The neighbor nodded in return. There was a look on his sharp narrow face that Jacob couldn't interpret, and then the family group turned a corner, the chattering fading away.

As Jacob approached the corner of his own street, he decided he wasn't thinking clearly about Isaac because of Miriam's involvement. He was as certain as he could be that Isaac had no other prospective husbands for Miriam, but it was likely someone with more wealth could offer a tribute directly to Isaac and a substantial bride price.

The thought churned his stomach, but Jacob shook his head, turned the corner and saw why his neighbor had given him such a strange look.

At the far end of the street, outside Jacob's house, were three men dressed in the richly decorated and flamboyant uniforms of the Temple Guard. On the left side, two of the men pressed close to the door of Jacob's house. Between them Jacob could make out the shape and clothing of Passhur, his house servant.

The third man stood off to the right and back several paces, his right hand resting on the hilt of his sword, his feet placed in such a way as to give him complete balance if he needed to draw the weapon. A professional, Jacob judged, and an officer from the look of the bright lines of gold thread woven into the white tunic that almost shone in the morning light.

There was something in the man's stance that triggered a memory, but Jacob was too far away to see the man's face clearly enough and know if he'd met the soldier before.

He focused his attention on the two soldiers crowding in on Passhur. Those two weren't professional, he noted as he moved forward, transferring his weight forward to the balls of his feet. They stood too close to Passhur, and too close to each other. There was no room to draw their weapons easily, let alone use them effectively.

Jacob felt his muscles tense. The churning worry about Miriam disappeared, replaced with a blossoming flutter of fear and excitement in his belly. He wasn't looking for a fight, but they could have one if they wanted. He didn't care if they reported to Arioch, or any of the other priests at the Temple of Marduk. Passhur was his responsibility.

He took another three paces forward, then called out.

"You there. Stop that. Leave my servant alone."

The two men stepped back, letting Passhur slump to the dirt and dust of the street as they turned to face Jacob. One short and overweight, his tunic straining across the belly. The other thinner and more hesitant in his movements. They both reached for their swords.

In the corner of his eye, Jacob sensed the officer turn as well, and noted he still hadn't drawn his sword. Two to one, and Jacob carried no weapons; not that it bothered him. In the last days of the siege of Jerusalem, there'd been few swords or knives left to the defenders. The night patrols Jacob led against the Babylonians had required creativity.

The two Temple Guards had drawn their swords, but they were still too close together. Part of it was the relative narrowness of the street, but the real reason, Jacob knew, was their inexperience. Staying close gave them a sense of mutual protection. A false sense because an experienced fighter, even one with a maimed right arm and no bladed weapon, like Jacob, could get close enough with his hands to slash and maim and injure.

Jacob selected the heavier man as his first target; the one closest to the wall. The man would have to move to his left to wield his sword properly, and that would cut across the path of the thinner man, blocking his sword arm. Just outside sword reach, Jacob would switch targets, take down the smaller man, snatch his sword and deal with the fat man and the officer.

Pebbles rattled together behind him, and Jacob heard the scrape of swords drawn from leather scabbards.

Passhur had risen to his knees, his dark eyes wide and pleading with Jacob, the wispy strands of gray hair waving from side to side as he shook his head.

Jacob glanced back and saw three more Temple Guards, swords drawn and spaced the correct way for close combat in a narrow street.

"It seems what you told me about the siege of Jerusalem weren't just tales intended to impress," the officer said, his voice deep and low, a half-smile on his full lips. "Although you know your proposed moves would leave your back exposed to me."

Jacob relaxed his posture, settling his weight back on every part of his feet. Two men he could handle. Five and the officer who he now recognized. That was expecting too much.

"Not long enough for you to do anything about it," Jacob said, with a smile of his own, although he wasn't feeling humorous. "There are better ways to seek me out, Zabium. Why is the commander of Arioch's personal guard bullying my servant?"

Zabium shrugged, his dark brown eyes flashing with what could have been amusement at Jacob's response. "He wouldn't tell us where you were, then tried to run."

"Five Temple Guards can't hold an elderly man whose back pains him every time the heat of the day fades away? You can do better than that, Zabium."

"I don't have to, Jacob. Priest Arioch wants you at the Esagila. It's important."

Behind Jacob, the three guards moved forward several paces.

"And not an option," Zabium added.

CHAPTER FIVE

The Babylonian New Year Festival
Day Five - Morning

Important, and not an option.

Jacob wondered what was so important that Arioch sent the commander of his personal guard to escort him to the Esagila. He gave a small shrug. He'd know soon enough.

"I have business commitments today. Let me send messages so I'm not considered rude."

"During the New Year Festival?" Zabium considered the request, then nodded. "Your people have many strange customs, Jacob. Be quick. You know as I do, that Arioch doesn't like being kept waiting."

Jacob crossed quickly to Passhur, helping the elderly man in the last stages of getting to his feet. The dust of the street had caked on his robe and the left side of his face, making his wispy brown hair look gray. There was a tear in the right sleeve of Passhur's robe, and the beginning of a swelling on his left cheekbone.

"The fat one, or the thin one?" Jacob asked, helping Passhur lean back against the wall to get his breath. Jacob positioned his body so none of the guards could see Passhur's mouth move.

"The thin one. From behind, so I had no chance of avoiding him."

Jacob nodded and took a long, slow breath to control the temper rising inside him. This wasn't the time or the place, but there would be a place and a time.

"Get yourself cleaned up, Passhur," he said evenly. "Then I need you to go to Isaac's home. Speak only to Isaac. Tell him they've escorted me to the Esagila at Arioch's request. I don't know why, but I'll visit the house as soon as I can. If I've not returned by sundown, make sure he asks questions." Jacob paused, wondering how to ensure Isaac followed through. He almost smiled when he realized his leverage.

"Tell Isaac the success of the Judah caravan may depend on this."

"And Bel Ibni?" Passhur asked. "Aren't you supposed to see him later today?"

"He can wait until tomorrow," Jacob told him with a reassuring smile, then turned back to Zabium, noting the rich strands of auburn hair on the shoulder of the Babylonian's tunic. "I'm ready. As you rightly say, it's not good to keep Arioch waiting. Is your wife well?" he asked.

Zabium frowned at him, and in doing so saw the long curls of hair on his clothing. He brushed them away. "She is well, although not pleased I have left our family during the Festival. And when Inanna is unhappy, everyone is unhappy."

Jacob had labeled the thin and fat guards as having little or no experience. They brought up the rear, while the three who had come up behind him were, Jacob decided, professionals like Zabium. It was those three who led the way as they began weaving through the side streets toward the Esagila, leaving Jacob and Zabium in the middle.

"Do you know what Arioch wants?"

"Your presence," Zabium said. "Anything more, he'll tell you himself." He deliberately looked away, then barked an order at the leading guards, who began walking faster, and calling ahead to make the other people on the streets move out of the way.

There was no way to get to the Esagila without crossing Processional Street, and the nearer they came to the Temple complex, the heavier the crowds, and the slower they moved. Everyone wanted to attend the ceremony where Nebuchadnezzar was divested of his royal garments, made to kneel, pray for forgiveness, and be slapped by the chief priest until tears flowed. The tears were supposed to be a good omen for the next year of the king's reign.

Privately, Jacob doubted the tears made any difference. He came out of his reverie when the three guards in front came to a stop, and he nearly walked into them. The street ahead was jammed with revelers, all trying to force their way onto Processional Street, which was maybe thirty paces ahead of them.

The leader of the front three guards looked back at Zabium, a question on his face. The chatter and singing and laughing of the crowd, and the shrill excitement of the children made normal speech impossible.

Zabium scowled, opened his mouth to say something, realized it would be pointless, and lifted his right hand, using palm and fingers to convey a message.

The man frowned back. He didn't like what he was being told, but he knew there was no option. He leaned close to the other two, spoke in their ears. They formed a small wedge and began pushing through the crowd, ignoring the complaints and elbows thrust at them.

Zabium stepped into the hollow of the wedge, with Jacob right behind him.

Slowly they pushed their way out onto Processional Street, and began angling across to the west side through the crowd that resisted their progress and cursed in accents from Kish, Nippur, other cities, and Babylon itself.

Finally, they reached the far side and paused under the towering walls surrounding the Esagila. Twenty paces along the wall, and in the same direction the crowd was moving, was a small gate. It took them moments to reach it, and the guard, recognizing Zabium, let them through.

They passed through a dark narrow passageway, the air cool and pleasant after the heat and crush of the crowds. At the far end another door led them out into the huge central courtyard of the Esagila: nearly two stadia wide, and almost three stadia long.

Jacob blinked, and shook his head, to clear the disorientation caused by the sudden open space, the bright light, and the blessed, relative quiet. He heard Zabium dismiss the guards, then the Babylonian turned to him.

"This way," Zabium said, and set off across the courtyard at a brisk pace, weaving between the small groups of priests, acolytes, and servants, going about their business like this was a normal day, instead of one of the most holy days in the Babylonian year.

Zabium was nearly two hand spans taller than Jacob, and Jacob had to resort to the fast march cadence from his soldiering days to keep up. He was almost panting when they reached the far side of the courtyard, went through a wide arch, and down a flight of wide stone steps.

In his previous visits to the Esagila, Jacob had been in the more public areas of the complex to the south near the Temple of Marduk. Now Zabium was leading him into areas most Babylonians never saw.

At the bottom of the stairway, they passed rows of storage rooms and animal pens as they wended their way deeper into the complex. The rank smell of the animals in the confined space made Jacob's stomach churn. The noise of bleating goats and squawking chickens made any conversation impossible.

From the first days of their Exile in Babylon, Jacob knew the Temple of Marduk was one of the largest traders in the city, but he'd never fully appreciated the scale of their business until now.

There was a continual stream of priests and clerks pushing and shoving their way along the hallways. Jacob saw identifying markers carved into the walls beside each room and tried to keep track of them in case he returned without an escort. The pace of Zabium's stride, and the dim lighting only allowed him to catch the occasional symbol.

Finally, they paused in a large chamber lit to near daylight brightness with sesame oil lamps that flared and guttered as people moved by, infusing the air with the nutty scent of sesame.

Zabium conferred in low tones with two guards who gestured toward an archway with more steps leading down.

As they descended, air moved up past them, cool and feeling damp on Jacob's arms. There were maybe forty or fifty steps before the stairs ended in another hallway, with ceilings three or four cubits above Jacob's head. Ahead of him, more oil lamps hung from brackets on the walls, and there was a heavy odor of sesame.

Doorways opened off the hallway. Arioch stood tall and erect outside one of them and turned as he heard Zabium's sandals slap on the floor. The priest's angular face and high cheekbones alternated between shadow and highlight as the lamps flickered.

The contrasts made him appear first human, then demonic. The hood of his scarlet robe was pushed back and unusually, he wasn't wearing the headpiece of a senior priest which allowed his dark hair to flow down onto the collar of the robe.

Arioch rarely bothered with pleasantries and waved his arm, showing the storage rooms. "We use these rooms for valuable goods. Yesterday, there was silver and olibanum stored here, intended as a tribute offering during the New Year Festival. This morning it's gone."

"It wasn't me," Jacob said.

Arioch's dark eyes sparked with anger, and Jacob sensed Zabium take a half-step away in case Arioch's temper couldn't be controlled.

"I know that or you'd be in a room on the level below this and begging to tell me all you know."

"How much silver?"

"Ten wooden crates. Each one is two cubits by four, and four sacks of the olibanum."

Jacob made some quick calculations in his head. Even half-full the value of silver in the crates would be substantial, and that was without the olibanum, which was worth a small fortune in its own right. He had a good sense of what Arioch was going to demand of him, so he continued the questions.

"Where did you get that much olibanum?"

"From a merchant I have contact with in Ur. He represents the Kingdom of Dm't. The delivery came up-river three days ago. Zabium commanded the escort that brought the sacks directly from the wharf to this room."

Jacob turned to the soldier. "Did anything unusual happen when you brought the olibanum here? I mean no insult, but could the bags have been tampered with during the journey?"

Zabium pursed his lips, and Jacob could almost see the man's teeth grind together. The Babylonian breathed deeply and shook his head. His voice when he spoke was even and controlled.

"His Excellency inspected the cargo on the vessel. When he was satisfied, my men brought the sacks here with an additional escort. There were four sacks. His Excellency and I oversaw every part of the operation. The cargo was in our sight all the time. No-one would have changed the contents of the sacks before they reached this room."

"These are men from my personal bodyguard," Arioch added. "They consider their selection a favor granted to them, and to their families. If any of them betray me, justice will include every member of their family."

Jacob had heard of the practice. Tiglath-Peleser, the king who ruled Assyria over a hundred years before, had bound his personal guard in the same way, but it was the first time he'd heard of a priest doing the same thing. It wasn't something Jacob wanted to have hanging over his head, and he was grateful none of the Judean kings had attempted the same way to enforce loyalty.

"What do you want from me?"

Arioch looked at Jacob, his dark eyes wide with apparent surprise, like he couldn't quite believe the question needed asking. "I want you to find out who took the silver and olibanum and get it back. The king returns from Borsippa tomorrow with the god Nabu. I want this matter resolved before we return the god Nabu to the Temple in Borsippa in seven days. The honor of this Temple is at stake."

"If it's Temple honor, you must allow me to investigate this crime," Zabium protested.

"I agree with Zabium," Jacob said. "This isn't what I do, Arioch. It's a Temple problem, and Zabium should be the person to find the thieves."

"You remember when Bel Ibni's son was accused of theft in this Temple?"

Jacob nodded. He felt his gut squeeze. He didn't like where Arioch was taking this conversation.

"That was as much for the Temple as it was for Bel Ibni, or Horam. You have a talent for finding answers, Jacob." Arioch's dark eyes seemed to become darker, almost black, and his lips compressed into a thin line. Jacob had seen the signs before and braced himself for an outburst. Instead, Arioch's voice was deadly calm, and that was almost more unnerving.

"Your people have made great strides in Babylon these past four years, Jacob. It would be a great shame if the freedom and privileges you've all gained were removed."

Arioch opened his clenched fist and dangled a length of blue cord from his fingers. He let it hang for a moment, then tossed it at Jacob. "This is all the evidence I need to send Zabium and his men into every house and place of business your people have in Babylon and surrounding villages like Kweiresh. There are plenty of Babylonians who would welcome the chance to run those farms and furnaces with your people as indentured servants. Or you can find out where that cord came from and with it my silver and olibanum."

"It should still be my investigation," Zabium protested again.

Arioch shook his head. "Not this time, Zabium. You won't get the information you need from Jacob's people, no matter how extreme your methods of persuasion. I believe it's called stiff-necked. Isn't that right, Jacob?"

"It has been said."

Finally, Arioch allowed his face to relax into an amused smile, and the blackness faded from his eyes. "That's settled, then. I expect the two of you to work together on this, and once it's settled, perhaps we can discuss your caravan to Judah, Jacob."

CHAPTER SIX

The Babylonian New Year Festival
Day Five - Morning

In the shadowy half-light of the sesame lamps, Jacob could see the tension in Zabium's stance as Arioch strode away, saying nothing more.

Jacob looked down at the strand of blue cord in his hand. It was slightly longer than the length from the tip of his thumb to the tip of his little finger. And old, the color faded so that in some places the blue was almost white. He rolled it between his thumb and forefinger, feeling the cord shift and bunch under the pressure, but not as much as he'd thought it might. It felt different from the cord on his own shawl. That cord was woven in Jerusalem, and he guessed this cord had been made somewhere else, probably here in Babylon.

"Where was this found?" he asked Zabium.

"It was against the far wall of the storeroom. Arioch recognized it and sent me to bring you here."

"It's a piece of blue cord. Why assume it belongs to one of my people? I've seen Babylonians, Persians, and Armenians wearing blue all over the city."

"As have I," Zabium agreed, then shrugged. "Usually I can follow the path of Arioch's thoughts. On this he's walking his own road, but I assume he had a reason for bringing you here."

Jacob thought so, too.

Arioch's action suggested he didn't completely trust anyone in the Temple to find the thieves. As commander of the guard, the silver and olibanum were Zabium's responsibility, and whatever the outcome of the investigations, there would always be a silent question hanging over his head. Was he involved, and if so, how? If Arioch allowed Zabium to lead the investigation, those questions could suggest Arioch was complicit.

Jacob sighed. It was hard enough building a life here in Babylon without becoming tangled in the politics of the Temple of Marduk. He rolled the cord through against his palm, feeling it slide a little under his grip. He looked down, surprised to see a sheen of oil on his fingers. It was bright in the flickering light of the torches and when he lifted his fingers to his nose. He expected the familiar nutty smell of sesame, but there was no odor he could detect.

"What is it?" Zabium asked.

"Nothing," Jacob said. "Or perhaps nothing I understand at the moment." He turned his attention to the doorway. "Was anything else moved in or taken out?"

Zabium shook his head. "There was nothing else in the room. Just the silver and the olibanum."

Jacob reached up and lifted one of the rush torches from the wall fitting with his left hand. He tested the weight, then transferred the torch to his weaker right hand and stepped toward the doorway of the storeroom.

The door frame was hardwood, mahogany probably, and Jacob wondered if it had been part of the cargo he'd sold to Arioch several moons before. The wood was stained deep red: a color the Babylonians believed protected them from evil spirits. Protection in the same way his people daubed their doorposts and lintels with the blood of the lamb every Passover.

The door was of the same wood and as thick as the distance from Jacob's wrist to his fingertips. The wood under his hand was still rough, and Jacob was careful to avoid a splinter. The door swung smoothly and silently when he pushed against it, the ironwork of the intricate lock assembly flashing brightly in the torch's light.

"Do you have a key for this door?" he turned his head toward Zabium.

"No," Zabium growled, and Jacob felt the other mans's frustration in that one word. "There's only one key for this storeroom. Arioch keeps it and carries it with him at all times."

Jacob nodded, and the torch flared and flickered as he moved all the way into the storeroom. It was perhaps ten cubits square and as many high. The floors and walls were stone blocks, cut and scoured to a smooth even surface. There were thin indistinct lines where the blocks fitted closely with no mortar. In the far corner there was a hole in the ceiling, maybe a cubit on each side. Jacob crossed the room and stood beneath it, feeling the soft movement of air touch his face.

"It's for ventilation," Zabium said, his body filling the doorway. "The Temple stores spices in these rooms. If the air doesn't move, the vapors can build up. Some years ago, we used closed storage rooms near the river. The Temple lost two promising novitiates when the dust exploded."

His voice was flat and without emotion, and Jacob wondered if he'd had any connection to those novitiates. There had been similar incidents in Solomon's Temple in Jerusalem, so Zabium's story didn't surprise him.

Jacob lifted the torch toward the shaft, raising it as high as his arm would allow and tilting his head back so he could see into the shaft. In the flickering light he saw a single course of dressed and smooth stonework, then the more familiar mud bricks. The mud bricks weren't laid as carefully, and he could see something caught on a protrusion.

"Find something I can stand on to reach that shaft," he said to Zabium.

"What have you found?"

"I'll tell you when I've looked more closely. Maybe nothing."

The Babylonian huffed with displeasure, but his sandals scraped on the floor, and Jacob heard his voice outside, barking for the servants and issuing orders.

The servants brought more torches, and a ladder made from the trunk of a date palm, the cross pieces tied in place with reeds. The top extended into the lower edge of the ventilation shaft. Two of the servants held the ladder steady, and Jacob climbed the first four rungs carefully, testing each step before committing his weight to the step above. On the fifth step, his head was level with the opening of the ventilation shaft.

Jacob reached down and took a fresh torch from a servant, balancing it in his right hand, then trusting to his balance, he reached up with his left hand and brushed his fingers over the protrusion he'd seen earlier. Dried mud and pieces of cloth flaked off the brick and he caught them in his palm, catching the scent of something recognizable.

He lifted the strands of cloth to his nostrils, capturing the rich resiny scent of olibanum; heady and intoxicating. The smell of it caught in Jacob's throat, making him catch his breath, his nostrils already constricting, the reaction making his eyes water. He felt his sense of balance shift and let the strands of cloth drop from his fingers as he reached up and placed his palm on the edge of the shaft to steady himself.

Jacob breathed deeply to clear the odor from his nose and risked going a step higher so his head was inside the shaft. His shoulders bumped against the edges and the faint smell of the olibanum was losing the competition with the damp air that drifted down the shaft.

He was too big to get any further into the shaft, so he stepped back down and looked into Zabium's upturned face.

"What have you found?" Zabium demanded again.

"Possibly the way your thieves entered and escaped. It looks like one of the olibanum bags caught on the stone and left pieces of the sack and shavings of the olibanum." Jacob climbed all the way down, retrieved the strands he'd dropped and offered them to Zabium.

The Babylonian guard commander lowered his head and sniffed carefully. When he stood straight, he nodded agreement and there was a triumphant look in his dark brown eyes. "It's olibanum. His Excellency will be pleased."

"Strands of sackcloth and a smell won't satisfy Arioch. He wants all four sacks and the silver back in his possession. If you don't know that, you've not worked for him long enough."

"You're right," Zabium admitted grudgingly, and there was something in his eyes. "This is a start, but not what he wants, or is expecting. What else do you need?"

"We can feel the air movement so the shafts must come out into the open air somewhere. How do we find out where?"

"There were plans, but we need permission to see them."

"Then get permission," Jacob said. "And the plans. There's nothing more I can do here until you, or Arioch get them. I also want to know who constructed the lock."

"The room was locked, and Arioch has the only key. I told you this."

Jacob pushed the strands of fabric into the pocket of his robe. "Then there won't be a problem giving me the name of the artisan. You know where to find me when you have what I need."

For a moment, Jacob thought Zabium was going to protest, but the other man shrugged, gestured at a servant, then changed his mind. "We'll begin with Arioch for the plans and the artisan. He'll be making preparations for the god Nabu later today."

They walked back along the hallway, retracing the way they had come. "I've been meaning to ask," Zabium said as they climbed the first set of stairs. "Your countryman, Eli, and his family. Are they still safe?"

"They are, but he's not happy with me."

"Jacob, you saved their lives."

"That was more you and your men," Jacob said as they made their way up the last flight of steps. "After Nidintu left, I convinced Eli to become our caravan master. He's afraid he's too visible in the event you left any of the bandits alive. Someone who might recognize him and exact revenge."

"There were no bandits left alive," Zabium said. "I understand you needed to replace Nidintu, and Arioch is open-minded enough to accept a Judean. Allowing one of your people to lead a caravan to Jerusalem is a step too far for many of the priests in the Temple. If you had a Babylonian to at least appear in charge, that would help you."

"I know that," Jacob said. "When I find someone who can handle the position, I'll let you know."

CHAPTER SEVEN

The Babylonian New Year Festival
Day Five - Afternoon

At the top of the steps from the storage rooms, both men paused and caught their breath. When they began walking again, Jacob expected Zabium to turn right and retrace the way they'd come earlier. Instead, the Babylonian turned left and took them along wide hallways with ceilings twice Jacob's height, weaving their way through a continual procession of priests, acolytes and other Temple workers, all dressed in rich colored robes. Most of them moved with an air of anticipatory excitement, ignoring the sculptures and richly colored tapestries that hung from the walls. Jacob saw more than a few walking carefully, heads down, eyes bloodshot, and faces ashen.

Zabium glanced at the sufferers and shared a grim smile with Jacob. "Even our priests celebrate a little too much sometimes." He pointed to an archway on their right. "Through here. It's the quickest way to reach Arioch."

A dozen paces along the new hallway, and they came out through a larger archway into the main courtyard of the Esagila.

After the dim and shaded light in the hallways, Jacob screwed his eyes closed at the explosion of bright daylight and wished he could have done the same for his ears.

What had been an almost empty space when Jacob arrived had become a seething mass of people. He suspected the courtyard could hold many more, but the noise from those already there was loud and shrill, with occasional spikes of angry shouting. It made the courtyard feel overly full.

Away to his left, Jacob saw drifting tendrils of smoke from a line of braziers where vendors had set up stalls to offer food. He could smell the burning palm chips, vegetables, and meat, almost taste it. His stomach growled in protest. Jacob remembered he'd planned to eat a proper meal at his home after Shema that morning. A plan that had changed with Zabium's arrival.

"Arioch is over there," Zabium gestured.

Jacob saw the Priest to the right, surrounded by a group of clearly unhappy citizens.

"He's dealing with lesser nobles and people who think their influence at court is greater than it really is. Each one of them believes their position in the procession to the Temple of the New Year Festival should be closer to the king."

"Maybe we can rescue him," Jacob said, leading the way through the press of people to where Arioch was taking a step back as a short fat man shuffled forward and continued haranguing the priest.

"My lord," Arioch was saying. "I cannot sit you that close to the king and have you at the front of the procession. It's just not possible."

"Do you know how much I contributed to the Temple in the last year?"

Arioch's barrel chest heaved under the robe as he took a deep breath, then his posture seemed to relax as he saw Zabium move into his line of sight.

"What is it, Zabium?"

"The landing stage, your Excellency. Some brickwork collapsed and damaged the statues of the gods waiting for Nabu to arrive."

"This is most serious," Arioch said. He turned back to the noble whose face had turned red with frustration at the interruption. "You must excuse me, my lord. If we do not attend to this matter, there may not be a procession."

Arioch gestured to one of the junior priests flanking him. For a moment, the young man looked stricken, his slender body rooted to the spot where he stood. Arioch placed a hand on the man's shoulder, said something, and stepped away.

Jacob was too far away to hear but saw the young priest smile, straighten his back and step into the fray.

"What's really going on?" Arioch demanded as they moved away through the crowd. "There are no statues on the landing stage."

Quickly Jacob told Arioch what they'd learned in the storeroom.

"Why do you need to see the plans?" Arioch asked.

"If the thieves used the air shafts to remove the silver and olibanum from the room, knowing where the shafts come above ground may help Zabium and I find where the silver is being stored."

Arioch frowned and said. "You don't sound very certain."

"I'm not, but right now, I have no other ideas."

The priest sighed and pinched the bridge of his nose. "The filing clerks work for Priest Subisha. They aren't known for their cooperation unless another priest provides some persuasion. Come with me."

They followed Arioch along another maze of corridors to a small chamber where a man sat hunched over a scribing table. Piles of clay tablets in various shapes and sizes surrounded him, and even more were stacked on the floor.

Jacob held back a step to keep away from the damp clay smell.

The scribe looked up when he heard their footsteps, his sharp features twisting into a scowl. He paused and put his stylus aside.

"What do you want?" he demanded.

"The scrolls showing the building plans for the lower level storage rooms," Arioch said. "We need to see them."

The clerk took a deep breath and pursed his lips in the same way Jacob had seen donkeys behave before digging their hooves in and refusing to move.

"I might arrange it after the New Year Festival. Priest Subisha has taken three of my staff on the journey to Borsippa. We're short-handed and our work doesn't stop just because it's another new year."

"I understand," Arioch conceded. "All I need is for you to take a quick break to explain the system to my colleagues. Once that's done, they can retrieve what we need from the archive."

The mulish stubbornness evaporated, and Jacob hid a smile. The clerk was fiercely possessive of his records. There was no way he would allow Jacob and Zabium into the archives on their own.

The clerk put the stylus to one side and stepped away from his desk. His arms and legs were like sticks placed awkwardly on his body and his ungainly walk, with the brown robe billowing around his thin body, reminded Jacob of the storks and herons he'd seen paddling the shores of Galilee.

"It's well past the time I should take a break anyway," he said and pointed a bony twig-like finger at Zabium and Jacob. "Come on, this won't take long."

He pointed toward a doorway covered with a tan-colored ox-hide, pushed the skin aside and waved for them to follow him. He led them into a long narrow room with high ceilings and rickety looking shelving that held hundreds, probably thousands of scrolls and clay tablets. Windows high in the wall allowed in blocks of bright sunlight that blazed in small rectangles and cast the rest of the room into semi-twilight. The windows surprised Jacob until he realized this wasn't a place where torches or oil lamps were wanted as a source of light. The air was musty and stale with the dry woody fragrance that came from the papyrus scroll, and the dry smell of dust from the clay tablets.

"We added those store rooms two or three years ago," the clerk chattered. "The locks Priest Arioch had installed are quite a step forward for the Temple."

Jacob remembered a conversation where Amos had mentioned the Babylonians documented everything. Only now, as the clerk led them along the stacks, did Jacob believe it. "How are your records organized," he asked.

The clerk's stride faltered for a moment and he turned, disbelief and horror on his face. "Do you not see the tablets attached to each shelf? They tell you what's there. It's based on the system from the library on Nineveh. The shape of the tablets tells you what the transaction represented; round for agriculture, four sides for business. There are rooms for history, law, government, and whatever else the Temple needs."

He stopped, the flapping robe coming to rest round his bony shoulders as he peered forward and squinted at a tablet. He nodded, a jerk of his upper body that again reminded Jacob of a stork, as the clerk moved a few paces further. He reached into a pile of scrolls, pulling one out and checking it, then selecting another.

"I know scrolls and papyrus are the future, but they're so untidy. You can stack tablets, and they're safer. Do you know how many tablets survived after the burning of the library at Nineveh? All of them. Not one scroll survived." He pulled two more scrolls from the stack, and there was something in his actions that sent a flutter of unease through Jacob's stomach.

"So, you can give us the scroll with the plan," Jacob said, glancing at Zabium and seeing concern on the Babylonian's face.

"Yes. I mean. . ." The clerk's voice trailed off. He pushed the scrolls back into the stock and checked the markings on the tablet tied to the racking with thin papyrus rope. "They should be here," he stammered, his face going pale. The certainty of his world was badly shaken.

"Could the scrolls be in another stack?" Jacob asked.

"That would be wrong," but there was no passion in his indignation and he searched the alcoves above, below, and on each side without success. "They should be here," he repeated, his voice cracking slightly.

"Who did the work in the storerooms?" Zabium demanded. "We can get copies from him."

"That's easy," the clerk said, life coming back into his voice along with the color to his cheeks. "This was work done for Priest Arioch, so it would have been Buvalu the brick maker. He's usually in and out of here all the time, but good luck getting him today, or for the next few days. He'll tell you he's working, but he makes the most of the New Year Festival."

"Where can we find him?" Zabium asked.

"His brick kiln is outside the Inner Wall. I think it's somewhere between the Marduk Street gate and the Nil Canal," he paused. "Well, there's nothing more to see here. Let's get you back outside. Perhaps His Excellency, Priest Arioch, can give you a more precise location. Meanwhile, I need to learn which lazy dog of a trainee is attempting to make a mockery of my filing system."

When Zabium relayed the story to Arioch, the priest didn't seem surprised.

"You'll find Buvalu in his workshop early in the morning, even during the New Year Festival. The workshop is four streets north of Marduk Street and backs onto the Nil Canal."

"I'll meet you at the Marduk Gate just before sunrise," Jacob said to Zabium. The soldier shrugged and grunted a reluctant consent.

They left the clerk in his own world and as they returned to the noise and clamor of the Inner Courtyard, Arioch put his hand on the sleeve of Jacob's robe, making him slow down.

Arioch pitched his voice low so any eavesdropper couldn't hear them above the tumult.

"One last thing," he said. "When you see him next, remind Bel Ibni that the Temple of Marduk handles all trading with the Temple of Sin in Harran. I, or should I say, the Temple of Marduk does not appreciate being usurped, especially given the special relationship the priestess at the Temple of Sin has with the king. And I want to see you again in three days, early in the morning, whether or not you've learned anything of value."

He released his grip and strode away before Jacob could respond.

CHAPTER EIGHT

The Babylonian New Year Festival
Day Five - Afternoon

After spending the morning working with Jacob's shawl on the balcony, Miriam decided she needed the brighter light in the middle of the courtyard to deal with the fringes and tassels. She'd sent a servant to the family of Samuel for the blue cord she needed.

She'd only asked one thing of Samuel after delivering Samuel's oldest child and clearing the mess from the boy's mouth and throat so he could breathe and live. It was that event that had changed the minds of many who did not believe Miriam had the talent or mind to be a midwife and healer.

Now the boy, Enoch, was a lusty, mischievous two-year-old. Every time Samuel saw Miriam, he insisted she could ask for anything. She could never explain he had already given her the most important thing. He had trusted her to bring his son into the world, and now the community of Exiles her trusted as well.

The length of cord, when it arrived, was the wrong shade of blue, but long enough that Miriam could replace the entire length on Jacob's shawl. She set out her yarns and bone needles on a table in the courtyard's shade, sitting on a stool and beginning her work. After several more hours, the bright light and close work made her eyes ache, and she sat back, kneading them gently with the heels of her palms.

When she'd finished rubbing, Miriam looked at the shawl critically. She could see where the cord kinked and twisted despite her attempts to make it lay flat. She'd have to unpick the cord and see Samuel herself to find a cord that would lay close to the wool without twisting and kinking.

It wasn't just the close needlework that had her unable to concentrate.

She'd still been working on the upper balcony when Jacob's servant, Passhur, arrived and delivered his message to Isaac. Even now, several hours later, she felt a cold squeeze in her stomach when she recalled Passhur's words in her mind. Miriam shook her head and began separating the blue cord from the shawl, careful not to snag the wool and pull a hole in the woven material: King Solomon's wisdom said if you believed in something it would happen. She didn't need to believe the Babylonian's would arrest and interrogate Jacob.

"Don't give up on that shawl," a deep voice said. "He'll need it in the morning."

Miriam looked up, startled for a moment, nearly sticking herself with the needle, letting the cord slip from her fingers and grabbing for it, saving it before it landed below in the courtyard's dust. For a large man who was often clumsy, there were times when Amos could appear from apparently nowhere.

"I'm sure he will," she replied automatically.

Amos shook his head, a smile softening the contradiction. He looked around to reassure himself there was no-one else in the courtyard. His voice dropped to a whisper. "You helped me when I made a fool of myself gambling and drinking. What you don't know is what Jacob really did for me."

"I know he and Nidintu searched the house of the rogue Iddin and took clay tablets to prove your real debt."

Jacob had given her those clay tablets and asked her to keep them safe. No one else knew she had them, although they were no longer in her possession. That had been the one thing she'd asked of Samuel. And now only Samuel knew the location of the tablets.

"Did he also tell you Iddin sold the debt to Tiglath, one of the Babylonian merchants who hate us? Jacob and Nidintu visited Tiglath at his home across the river in the New City. I don't know what happened there, or who threatened who, but Jacob walked away with my debts cleared. I have no idea what I really owe him, or what Arioch wants or expects from him, but I know Jacob will be here in the morning. If he needs any help from me, whatever it is, I'll give it to him," he paused and laughed. "Just about anything's better than what I'm doing at the moment."

From his tone, and the way he'd sought her out, Miriam sensed he needed to talk. She folded the shawl and placed it in her bag with the yarn. Carefully, she folded a piece of thick cloth around the needles. As a younger woman, Miriam had stuck herself so many times it was a miracle the ends of her fingers weren't a mass of scars. When she'd placed the pack of needles in the bag, she turned her attention back to Amos.

"So, what are you doing, Amos? You leave here each morning soon after Shema and you don't return until late in the afternoon. Are you gambling again?"

He chuckled, the folds of flesh on his large body shaking with the amusement.

"Nothing like that, although sometimes it feels like it. You've heard Isaac talk about how Ezra wants to preserve our history and tradition? I'm sitting with the priests and story tellers and writing the stories of Abraham and Joseph and David. I tell you, listening to the priests argue over which version of Adam's story is the correct one, or whether David hid from King Saul in a barn or a cave is an experience. It's enough to drive anyone to drink."

"Is it so hard for them to agree?"

"Apparently, but I believe we should capture all the variations, and we can argue who's right later. Maybe they're both right. Maybe the cave was also a barn. But let's get our tradition on tablets and scrolls in case we never return to Jerusalem and in time lose our priests and story tellers. That's a bigger danger to our faith than a few people deciding Marduk might be a better god. We dealt with that issue in the desert when Moses brought the Commandments down from the mountain and some fool decided images of calves were better than the Yahweh who brought us out of Egypt, but you can't ever say we aren't stiff-necked."

Miriam couldn't help herself. She laughed, sat back on the stool, and shook her head, pushing a loose strand of dark hair back off her face. "Stiff-necked is part of who we are, Amos. You, me, Isaac, Jacob, and all of us Exiles. We might not even be in Babylon if we hadn't inherited that stiff-neck from before the time we left Egypt."

He spoke again, and as he did so, there was a movement across the courtyard; Solly coming in from the street door and a dark shadow following him.

Whatever Amos was saying became a noise that washed over Miriam unheard. She stood, the stool falling away behind, her heart suddenly beating harder as Jacob moved forward into the light of the courtyard. He turned his head as if he felt her gaze on him. His dark eyes sparkled for an instant, and the lines on his forehead smoothed away. He reached forward and touched Solly on the shoulder, saying something to him, then crossing the courtyard toward her.

Amos saved her, thanks be. He stepped forward and embraced Jacob.

"I was telling Miriam that Arioch wouldn't dare throw you in one of his dungeons. And that you'd be here for Shema tomorrow. Besides, I need you to keep telling me your stories, Jacob. How will our soldiers know what to do after we return from Exile if you don't pass on everything you know?"

Jacob slid his healthy left arm around Amos. He returned the hug and squeezed hard, his chin on Amos's left shoulder, his eyes focused on her.

"I have not forgotten the promise I gave you, although there are many of our soldiers here. Some of them are even officers in the Babylonian Army," Jacob said, his eyes never leaving her. "Arioch needs my help. I wanted Isaac to know I'm not in those dungeons and that I must offer my apologies for Shema tomorrow. I have to be in the Outer City as soon as the gates open so I can get information from an artisan who does work for their Temple." He shrugged in apology. "It's not what I want, but there's more happening than I know at the moment."

"What help does Arioch need?" Amos asked. "Other than a steadying hand after he's finished a jug of wine."

"There are some items missing and they found this in the room." He held up the short length of frayed blue cord. "I think it's a coincidence, but Arioch believes it involves our people."

"Can't you see this artisan later in the day?" Miriam asked.

Jacob smiled and shook his head. "If I leave it any later, he'll be deep into their New Year celebrations and unable to give coherent answers."

"You'll be missed," Miriam said, surprised at how calm her voice sounded. "However, it gives me the chance to make proper repairs to your shawl. I know it's dear to you, but you must take better care of it in the future," and then a thought came to her. "I want to visit Samuel tomorrow. I can repair the cord on your shawl, but it makes much more sense to replace it. Would you let me take the length of cord Arioch found? I can show it to Samuel, and perhaps he can tell us who made it."

She saw the change on Jacob's face as he considered her offer for a moment, then he nodded and handed the frayed cord to her. "That's a good idea. Take Amos or Solly with you. Some revelers forget their manners once they've had a drink or two, even the morning after."

CHAPTER NINE

The Babylonian New Year Festival
Day Six - Morning

The wide thoroughfare of Marduk Street ran from the Esagila to the Inner City gate, then north through the Outer City walls and northeast to Sippar.

The Marduk Gate didn't have the imposing grandeur or artwork of fantastic animals on a backdrop of shining blue tile to compete with the newly constructed Ishtar Gate on the northern approaches to Babylon, but it was more important to the city.

The Marduk Gate was the primary entry point for many of the workers who came into the Inner City each morning from the settlements sprawled between the gates and the outer defensive walls.

A massive gate house dominated the eastern end of Marduk Street, the stone walls reaching a hundred courses above the main city wall. The gate house itself guarded a tunnel that stretched for over a hundred paces under and through the city walls. At the far end, bronze gates gave access to the walkway alongside the canal.

Even during the day the tunnel was in permanent twilight, and at this early hour before the sun had fully risen it was dark and shadowy. The gate was designed and built to break up an assault on the city. Inside the tunnel the air was stale and damp, heavy with the smell of animals. The few people alongside Jacob talked in low voices, except for the occasional rough curse when someone inadvertently stepped into one of the foul-smelling puddles that trapped the unwary or careless.

The whole gate complex reminded Jacob of the Sheep Gate in Jerusalem, where he'd frequently commanded the guard. He had a good idea of what the defenders stored in the roof above his head and the devastation it could unleash on an attacker if they tried to invade Babylon through the Marduk Gate. He shivered and lengthened his stride, hurrying to get through and out into the light on the walkway by the canal.

There was a thin band of lighter sky on the eastern horizon as Jacob emerged from the tunnel, but it was still a while before sunrise, and the secondary gates giving access to the canal bridge remained closed. It surprised Jacob how many people were waiting to cross back to the Outer City. Groups of men ranging in age from youths to the elderly lounged on the ground or stood in small groups. Some moved with careful precision, their faces showing the ravages of too much wine or barley beer. There were family groups as well, people who'd probably stayed overnight to hear the Babylonian creation story, very different from the story Jacob and his fellow Judeans held sacred.

Zabium stood alone and aloof, his back against a corner of the city wall. His gaze flickered across the guard towers and the people waiting in a repeated cycle of watchfulness. His right hand rested on his stomach, but it would be a minimal movement to have the sword out of the scabbard on his left hip, the sword's hilt partially hidden by the long cloak Zabium had wrapped around himself. Jacob wasn't sure he liked the man; probably didn't but from what he'd seen, Zabium was a good soldier and he could respect that.

"There are more people than I expected," Jacob said as an introduction, although he was certain Zabium had seen him come out of the gate tunnel, and watched his approach.

"It's the New Year Festival. By the time we return the statue of Nabu to Borsippa after the final banquets, there'll be dozens sleeping out here, mostly hung over. The guards won't want them inside the city, but they'll not risk opening the gates to the bridge either. Have you met Buvalu?"

Jacob shook his head. "No. You?"

"Not formally, although we've seen each other in the Temple. In our language, his name means giant, and he has the size and temperament to match. Arioch tolerates him because he does excellent work. Buvalu hires a lot of your people because they're cheaper and he can work them harder."

The same cycle of events we endured in Egypt, Jacob thought; before Moses led us to freedom. He doubted there would be a similar Exodus from Babylon.

There was movement on the gate tower and Zabium stood straighter, his cloak pulling back. Jacob saw the rich purple tunic and a fringe of heavy gold tassels.

"No armor?" Jacob asked.

Zabium shook his head. "I said I've seen Buvalu at the Temple. He may not remember me so I want something that encourages him to cooperate and not make him feel intimidated."

Zabium gestured at the four guards who'd come out of the Marduk Gate and were crossing to the canal gates. A murmur of anticipation rustled through the crowd, and people began edging forward. "Come on, they're getting ready to open the bridge gates."

Jacob and Zabium were among the first group across the bridge. The span ended in an open space of scrub and sand, the nearest buildings another twenty or thirty paces away. It seemed strange until Jacob recognized it as more of the defensive thinking the Babylonians always seemed to consider as they built or extended their cities. There was no cover for a potential attacker close to the bridge. The open space also provided a staging area for those waiting to come into the inner city each morning, and already there was a crowd of carts and travelers waiting to cross the bridge.

Arioch's directions and Zabium's assessment of Buvalu were both accurate. The description of the place as a workshop was an understatement. Walls as tall as Jacob and half as high again, stretched for fifty paces on each side of the open gateway. As they entered through the gate, Jacob saw a kiln off to the left. He could feel the heat radiating from it as four workers moved mud bricks from a pile into the kiln. On the far side, there were head high stacks of bricks already baked. Behind the stack of bricks were blocks of rough stone, and Buvalu himself; a huge bull of a man, maybe a cubit taller than Zabium, and with arms bigger than most men's thighs.

Buvalu was bellowing at his workers as they moved bricks from the kiln to cool. He leaned forward and cuffed the closest worker, urging him to work faster. His movements stilled as a sensed their presence. He turned, frowned, and glared at Jacob and Zabium.

"What do you want?" he demanded.

"Artisan Buvalu, we are from Priest Arioch," Zabium said. "Where can we talk?"

"Arioch, eh? That means you want something. How do I know you're from Arioch?" he stabbed a finger toward Zabium, then folded his arms across the broad expanse of his chest, tilted his head to the left. "You look familiar from my time at the Temple, but I'll need more proof than my memory. Your friend isn't a priest or a soldier. He looks Judean to me. What use does Arioch have for him?"

"Many things that don't concern you," Zabium said, letting his cloak fall open to reveal his ornate uniform, and the gleaming bronze medallion that hung from a thin chain onto his chest.

Zabium tapped the bronze with his fingernail, and it made a soft ringing sound. "This is Arioch's seal. As Arioch's guard commander, I am trusted to wear it and ask questions as he would if he were here."

Buvalu straightened his head, pursed his lips, then shrugged. "We can talk here. These are Judeans, most of them barely understand our language, so it doesn't matter what you say."

"You built store rooms for Arioch two summers ago. We need to see the drawings."

Buvalu laughed then, a deep booming roar that made the workers pause and look up; some of them fearfully as if they expected more blows. "Arioch doesn't have his own?"

"The archives are being reorganized," Jacob said. "It's quicker to ask for your copies, especially during the New Year festival."

That got a reaction, but not from where Jacob expected. Several of the workers paused again, their heads twisted, giving Jacob hard looks as they recognized his accent.

"Aren't you one of them?" Buvalu jerked his head toward the workers.

"The drawings," Zabium interrupted, his voice harsher. "Once we have those, everyone can go back to celebrating the festival."

Buvalu sighed: a long explosion of breath. "Very well. Come with me."

There was a small room built against the wall on the far right-hand side of the compound; about as far away from the kiln as possible. There were no windows, and even at this early hour, the inside was hot and stifling. Scrolls and tablets were stacked haphazardly on shelves and the floor.

He must have had a system, Jacob thought, because Buvalu didn't hesitate. The brick maker reached through to the far wall and shuffled his hands through a set of scrolls, tipping his head to one side and squinting in the half-light at dark marks on the outside of each piece of pale-yellow papyrus.

After several minutes of searching, he straightened and turned to them. "They're not here," he said.

"Could the plans be somewhere else?" Jacob asked.

Buvalu's look was one of contempt. "And where would that be? You've seen where we work. Anything not in here is likely baked into a brick or in the pile of ash we haul away every day." He glared at Zabium. "Tell Arioch to impose some discipline on his clerks. I no longer have copies."

"Arioch will remember this," Zabium growled and pushed his way out of the building, leaving Buvalu holding a scroll and a sneer that twisted his face.

Jacob followed more slowly, his attention on the unlikely coincidence of both sets of plans being misplaced at the same time as the theft. A shadow across his path and a scrape of feet on the earth made him pause and realize two of the kiln workers were blocking his way.

The taller of the two was nearly a cubit taller than Jacob, his beard trimmed close to his chin, the rope of straggling brown hair tied back off his face and freckled with dust and pieces of mud brick. "Feel good about what you're doing?" he said in Aramaic, his enormous arms folded across his chest, displaying a ridged pattern of burn scars that ran from his wrist to his shoulder.

"What do you believe I'm doing?"

"Being their willing slave." The man spat in the sand at Jacob's feet. "Their law shackles us to Buvalu and his people with no options. But in here," he tapped his right hand over his chest. "In here, we're free, and we don't compromise." He spat again. "And we don't forget."

CHAPTER TEN

The Babylonian New Year Festival
Day Six - Morning

The sun had risen above the walls of the city when Miriam set out with Solly as her escort. She had packed a small basket with some herbs and small jars of salves for Samuel's family. The winter had been colder than usual and many young children in the Inner City had been ill; sneezing, coughing, and struggling to breathe. It didn't seem to have reached the Outer City with the same intensity, and with spring coming early this year, she hoped the illnesses would burn itself out before reaching the community of Exiles where Samuel lived.

As they reached Marduk Street, Miriam felt the sun's warmth through her robe, the heat on her body becoming uncomfortable. She'd considered changing from her brown heavy winter robe to the lighter, cooler summer one, but decided against it. The summer robe was showing signs of wear and hard use. She'd patched it more than once last year and hoped to get one more season before having to replace it. It was a decision she was regretting. While the lighter robe was adequate for the confines of Isaac's house, it wasn't acceptable for visiting the other Exiles, and this wasn't an occasion for wearing her best robe: the dark red one with the white needlework around the cuffs.

She shifted the basket as they entered the tunnel at the Marduk Gate leading under the city walls and out to the bridge over the canal. Now she was grateful for the heavier robe. A damp chill came off the bricks and in the semi-darkness, Miriam imagined she could see a damp, sour smelling mist rising from the stone floor.

Behind them a child cried in fear at losing the light, its wail echoing hollowly along the walls and roof before fading away into a muffled sobbing. The general chatter and sense of joy from the Babylonian revelers disappeared as well. Their voices fell to a hushed murmur and their footsteps lengthened and the pace quickened. Miriam joined them, thankful for the hurry and relief at reaching the light at the far end, even though it meant the heat of the day back on her robe.

By the time they arrived at Samuel's home, her undergarments were damp with perspiration and the robe seemed to cling to her in all the wrong places.

Unlike Isaac, many of the Exiles couldn't afford to live in the Inner City of Babylon and had congregated in small communities in the Outer City. Samuel's house was in a community that lay to the south of the Sippar Road and close to the outer walls, still four times a man's height, that guarded the Outer City.

The house was on a single level, a sprawling mud-brick building that looked over a large open courtyard with plenty of room not just for tables, but also space for couches where the family could gather before or after eating. Miriam loved the extra space in these houses. She didn't feel the walls closing in on her as she did at Isaac's home, and there was light here rather than the continual shade of the court-yards in the city. There was a group of palms on the east side of the house, and under their shaded foliage, several apple trees, and below them patches of greenery that would be the fresh onions, leek and cucumbers Samuel took great pride in cultivating.

Miriam shook the thoughts away as Samuel's wife, Rebecca, came toward them from the vegetable patch, brushing soil and twigs from her robe. There were silver strands in Rebecca's black hair and her body felt bony and just a little too thin as wrapped she her arms around Miriam to hug her, her head barely coming to Miriam's shoulder.

"I was telling Samuel just yesterday it was too long since we've seen you, Miriam. I said to him. I said, Samuel, if she doesn't visit soon, Enoch will walk into the city to find her."

"I've been meaning to come for some time," Miriam said. "But I wanted to avoid any chance of bringing the sickness. Did Enoch miss it?"

Rebecca nodded, taking Miriam's arm and pulling her between the tables toward the longer couches; guiding Miriam to one, then sitting so the two women were side by side. "We were luckier than many. There were a few coughs and sniffles, but nothing a good covering of cloaks and blankets couldn't cure. What was the need that made you take the chance and come to us?"

"First, I thought it was safe. Isaac's sons have been well for nearly a week, and the gossip says more people are getting better rather than becoming ill. The shawl cord Samuel sent yesterday wouldn't lay flat, so I'm hoping he has something else. And I need his knowledge. Well, Jacob needs it really, to see if we can find the person who made another piece of cord. I have it in my basket, and there's something for you."

Miriam reached into the basket and handed over the packages of herbs and jars of salves. "These will help if the coughs don't go away quickly."

"Bless you. It always helps to be prepared," Rebecca said, gathering the gifts together and standing. "You stay here while I get Samuel. I know he's not very busy at the moment. All the Babylonians are celebrating their New Year. Afterward, they'll want many repairs or new robes."

Samuel joined them as Rebecca brought out dates and a full skin of wine. He was a short man, barely a hand span taller than his wife, and so thin he looked like a strong wind would knock him down, except Miriam had seen the strength of the muscles in his skinny arms, when he'd single-handedly wrestled a collapsed weaving loom off the chest of one of his Babylonian workers.

"What do you need help with?" he asked, sitting on the couch opposite and wiping his hand through his thinning gray hair, then pouring wine for them.

"Two things," Miriam said. She pulled the original from Jacob's shawl from the pocket of her robe. "This came from a prayer shawl I'm repairing. The cord you sent yesterday is good, but it won't lay flat with the shawl. I was hoping you might have something else I could use."

"It must be an important shawl. Or an important person?" Rebecca added with a soft smile. A smile that grew broader as Miriam felt the flush heat her face. "I'll expect to hear more later."

Samuel smiled kindly at Miriam's embarrassment and took the length of blue cord from her. He rolled the cord through his fingers, letting his thumb nail dig in and tease apart the individual strands. A look of intense concentration came over his face.

"This is excellent quality," he said finally. "We don't have the expertise here in Babylon to make cord anywhere near as good as this. However, I have another length of blue shawl cord. It came from one of our military officers who died on the trek from Jerusalem. It may even come from the same artisan." His fingers rubbed again at the length of cord in his hand, and he seemed almost reluctant to return it to Miriam.

"You mentioned two things," Samuel said.

Miriam took out the piece of cord Jacob had given her. "This may be from a prayer shawl. I can't say too much. Jacob found it where you wouldn't expect to find a prayer shawl. I suspect it comes from Babylon and wondered if you could tell me anything more about it."

"Like who made it, and for whom?"

"That would be an unexpected, but pleasant surprise," Miriam said.

"There aren't many artisans making cord with the quality we expect for our shawls," Samuel said as his fingers repeated their inspection process on the new piece of cord. "It's not the cheapest, the quality is average. I don't mean to sound superior because I know some of our people can barely feed themselves. If this came from a shawl, it was very cheap, but I'm not sure it's cord for a shawl."

He pulled the cord tight between his hands and leaned forward, studying closely. "It's definitely a Babylonian weave," he said, his voice barely above a whisper as he relaxed his grip and began teasing the threads apart. "This comes from no one I deal with. I know their styles and patterns. I don't recognize this workmanship, but from the style, my guess would be it comes from the community at Kweiresh. It may be our people, but I can't be sure." He lifted his head and his intense brown eyes focused on Miriam. "There are some people I know in Kweiresh, and I can ask some questions. Or not. It's your decision."

"Not yet, but thank you." Miriam said. She wanted to talk with Jacob before asking Samuel to do something that could be dangerous.

"What do I owe you?" Miriam asked as Samuel stood, ready to return to his work.

"Nothing," Samuel raised a hand to stop her protest. "You brought Enoch into this world and saved his life. That is a debt our family will always owe you. Now, I'll find that cord while you catch up on gossip with Rebecca."

As he left, Rebecca shifted closer, her gaze fixed on Miriam. "The first cord. The one you want replaced. Is it for Jacob?"

Miriam nodded, feeling the color rise to her cheeks again. It seemed she had few secrets from her friends.

Rebecca smiled and reached forward to pour more wine. "He's a good man."

CHAPTER ELEVEN

The Babylonian New Year Festival
Day Six - Morning

Jacob returned the hard stares of the two brick workers as they moved closer. There was was no sign of Buvalu, and the other workers remained focused on their tasks. Both men were heavier and more muscular than he was. With his injury weakened right arm, Jacob knew there could only be one result if the conversation turned violent.

"Do you think the yoke and shackles that chain me are any less than yours?" he said. "One wrong word or thoughtless action, and the few freedoms we've gained in these last years will disappear like wheat chaff in a strong wind."

Jacob tapped his right hand on his chest as the other man had done. "I am also free in here, and I don't forget either."

Slowly, deliberately, Jacob turned away from both men and walked to the entrance of the brickyard.

When Jacob came out of the brickyard into the dusty street, he released the breath he'd been holding. Zabium hadn't waited and was far ahead, beyond the high wall that surrounded the brickyard, and almost back to Marduk Street. Jacob considered his options and decided not to catch up to the Babylonian.

To attempt it would allow the man to think Jacob was following his lead, and after the confrontation with Buvalu's Judean workers, Jacob felt the need to assert his own independence.

As Jacob reached Marduk Street, instead of turning toward the Inner City, he turned left, away from the Marduk Gate, and toward the Outer Gates of the city. The principal streets here were narrower, the mud-brick houses larger than those inside the city walls, more widely spaced, and with small plots for growing barley and vegetables. He crossed the secondary canal using the Nil Bridge.

There was a community of Judeans here, mostly artisans and craftsmen who couldn't afford homes in the city proper, and the houses clustered around the road that led north to Sippar. It was where his friend Samuel lived. Jacob considered an impromptu visit, changed his mind and kept walking.

Beyond the houses, and still inside the outer walls of the city, was the complex of stables, storehouses and sleeping quarters for caravans that were the major source of Babylon's wealth.

It also gave Jacob the chance to meet once more with Eli, the new caravan master, who was probably struggling to keep his men sober, and prepared for the journey. As a Judean like Jacob, and also a married man, Eli had little interest in the wild celebrations of the Babylonian New Year.

As Jacob approached the complex, he could hear the noise of donkeys braying, people shouting and cursing. When he reached his destination in the midst of the chaos, Jacob saw the big broad bulk of Eli himself, his long black hair whirling behind him as he moved to calm an animal, cuff a handler who was a pace too slow, or praise another man who had dragged a donkey away from the melee. He handed the halter of a struggling donkey; a jenny, to another man as if it were a foal, turned and saw Jacob.

The scowl on Eli's dark face twisted into a broad grin, making his forbidding face seem open and welcoming.

"Jacob," he called, and his face twisted into a wide smile. His long, lean body covered the distance between them in a few loping strides, and the two men clasped hands in greeting. "Have you finally come to do a day's work like an honest man?"

"Not likely," Jacob answered with a smile of his own. Eli had truly blossomed since Jacob had rescued him and his family from the clutches of a local bandit.

"I came to see how serious you are about setting out for Asshur tomorrow?"

Eli swept his arm across the area to encompass the surrounding men. "It will keep them from drinking too much and gambling away money they don't have. And we'll get a two-day head start on the other caravans heading north."

"And the onward journey to Nineveh?"

Eli frowned and waved to his wife, Rachel, to bring them drinks. "You're sure you want to go there? From what I heard, there isn't much left since the Babylonians and their allies burned and looted the city."

"That was thirty years ago, Eli. They might welcome the opportunity for some proper trade again. It's only two or three days of additional travel each way."

"I can probably do better than that," Eli said. A donkey brayed in protest, and he turned to watch the men calm it down. "We'll be in Asshur for at least a week. There are one or two men I can trust to handle the negotiations. That will allow me to go further north, and see just how bad, or good, the situation is in Nineveh."

"I like that idea," Jacob said, then switched the conversation to the other topic that bothered him. "Has Bel Ibni asked you to stop at the Temple of Sin on your way."

"No. Although some men have asked about it. From what I can

understand, it seems Nidintu had quite a lucrative alternate business on those visits. Did Bel Ibni talk to you about it?"

Until a month before, Nidintu, Bel Ibni's cousin, had been the caravan master. Nidintu, resenting his cousin's success, had attempted to undermine Bel Ibni.

A plot that had torn the family apart and left Jacob with several bruises.

The physical bruises had healed within a week, but the deeper scars in his soul still had Jacob questioning why he hadn't seen the warning signs. Jacob had considered Nidintu a good friend, still did, if he was honest. He'd arranged for Nidintu to travel away south to the city of Erech, and he hoped the man had conquered the demons that drove him.

Jacob wished Nidintu was here now, because the events at the Esagila had triggered a memory and he knew Nidintu would have the answer. It frustrated him he could think of no-one else to ask.

Jacob dragged his thoughts back to the present and shook his head. "Arioch delivered a warning yesterday morning. Bel Ibni's been avoiding me for the past two weeks, but I need him to hear about this."

Eli gestured at a group of couches, and low tables set in the shade of the stables. "You look thirsty, Jacob. We can talk over there."

"If it makes you feel any better, Bel Ibni's avoiding me as well," Eli said, after they made themselves comfortable on the couches and Eli's wife, Rachel, had poured generous helpings of the thin Babylonian barley beer into bronze mugs. "I think having another Judean in an important position worries him."

Jacob sipped and felt the tart flavor of the beer bubble across his tongue. It wasn't his favorite, but it was fresh and less likely to cause sickness than much of the water in and around the city.

"Most likely," Jacob agreed. "And I'm sorry to put you in this position. Our agreement was to keep you hidden until the caravan left for Judah." He took another sip of the tart liquid and changed the subject. "Do you know how many caravans Bel Ibni sent to Harran?"

Eli shook his head. "Definitely one, maybe two. He's working with people I don't know, which isn't hard given how new I am here. It was coincidence I found out; the lead handler bragged about his new side business."

"Did you talk to Bel Ibni about it?"

"My job here is hard enough. I don't need more conflict into my life, Jacob. Find a Babylonian to replace me when you can. It will make both our lives so much easier."

Jacob nodded as he sipped at the beer. Eli was just the last in a line of people who'd said, or implied, making Eli caravan master was a poor decision.

Jacob sipped again, still trying to work out what other options he'd had. He hadn't, and he knew it. So did Bel Ibni, if the Babylonian was being honest, but that didn't help either of them, and Jacob was almost grateful for the sudden commotion erupting behind him.

A group of donkeys were braying and complaining, and the handlers milled around shouting and waving their arms, reaching tentatively for the halters trailing in the dust.

Eli was halfway to his feet, then shrugged and sat back. "They think they're better at handling the animals than some Judean. Let them prove it."

He'd barely sat down when there was another commotion. Eli growled his displeasure and got to his feet again.

This time it wasn't handlers or donkeys.

Huba, Bel Ibni's elderly and unsteady door guard was tottering between the animals, snatching the sleeve of his robe away from snapping jaws and dancing away from the stamping hooves with an agility that surprised Jacob.

He saw them and gained a purpose in his direction.

"Jacob, I'm so glad you're here," he wheezed as he reached them. He pressed his bony fingers against this stomach and took several deep breaths that brought the color back to his cheeks. "I heard you left the city early this morning, and didn't know where

else to look, so I tried here. Come quickly. Someone attacked Bel
Ibni."

CHAPTER TWELVE

The Babylonian New Year Festival
Day Six - Afternoon

It was still early enough that many of the New Year revelers hadn't finished sleeping off the excesses of the previous evening. It would be midday before the second wave of revelers began congregating around the Esagila to welcome the royal barge back from Borsippa.

Jacob and Huba made good time back into the city, and then to Bel Ibni's home. Huba ushered Jacob through the street door and into the courtyard before returning to his guard post.

Jacob was grateful that King Nebuchadnezzar's ambitious plan to rebuild Babylon in its former glory had left no time for imaginative construction. The layout of each house and the building materials used were all very similar. Spending time at his own home, or Isaac's, or that of Bel Ibni, required little in the way of re-orientation. Jacob could stand inside the street door and look through the vestibule to the courtyard and know how to get to each of the rooms in the house.

There were variations, but they followed the same basic patterns. Where Jacob left space, Isaac constructed additional sleeping rooms to give Miriam and Amos privacy. In Bel Ibni's home, the merchant had built storage rooms, and a room dedicated to his business.

Bel Ibni's oldest son, Horam, was waiting in the courtyard. He was slight for his eighteen years, but what he lacked in muscle he made up for with determination. He was pacing slowly back and forth, and when he saw Jacob, he quickened his pace and came to Jacob, the tan robe billowing behind him. There was worry in his brown eyes, but he held himself straight and his voice was firm.

Jacob had watched him grow over the past few years and knew Horam was more than ready to start his own household.

"My father is in the business room, and a healing priest is with him." Horam said, then moved closer and lowered his voice. "I would have preferred the lady, Miriam, to attend my father, but those decisions are not mine to make."

Jacob smiled with sympathy and squeezed Horam's shoulder in gratitude. "Perhaps we can have her look at him in a day or two. Can I see your father?"

Horam nodded, and as they crossed the courtyard, he turned to face Jacob. "I don't know the cause of your differences with my father, Jacob, but please try to put them aside. I want you to attend my wedding."

"I'll do what I can. I'd like to be at your wedding as well. Do you know what happened today?"

He shook his head. "He intended to meet a merchant from Harran at the Temple of Ishtar so they could avoid the crowds watching the cleansing of Nabu's shrine. I don't know if the attacked happened on his way there or coming back." Horam offered a weak smile. "You know how he is when he doesn't want to answer a question."

Jacob nodded. He knew.

At the doorway. He ducked his head and walked under the red painted lintel into the small passageway that led to the sleeping rooms on that side of the house. He turned right and pushed through the double layer of cured ox hide that shielded the room from the rest of the house.

Light streamed in from the window high on the wall to the right, making the room bright and highlighting the shrine to Bel Ibni's gods on the far side of the room. Two wooden couches stood under the window, and Bel Ibni lay on the nearest one. Blood oozed from abrasions on his left cheek and there were tears in the tan colored robe covered in dirt and more streaks of blood.

The priest-healer was standing over Bel Ibni, hands on his hips. He turned as Jacob came into the room, the exasperation plain on his sallow face, and in his tone. "Who are you? Never mind. If you can talk some sense into this man, I don't care."

"Better people than you and I have failed at that," Jacob said, studying the tears on Bel Ibni's robe. "Is he having any difficulty breathing?"

"No. It only hurts when I turn to the left," Bel Ibni grumbled.

"Are you coughing up any blood? Do you have a headache?" Jacob pressed.

"The only headache I have is you," Bel Ibni growled. "I should get an actual door for this room. One made of wood, like they have in the Esagila, then you can beat your head against it while I decide who can enter."

The priest addressed Jacob. "What do you know of healing?"

"Enough to patch up battlefield wounds and keep people alive."

"Why ask about his head?"

"Strange things can happen to soldiers who've taken blows on the head, even when they have the protection of a helmet," Jacob said. "Sometimes there's nothing, then there are the ones who can't see properly for a day or two, others spend days not knowing where they are, and occasionally they'll get drowsy, go to sleep and never wake up."

"I've seen that happen," the priest said. "Can you do anything for them?"

"Watch for the drowsy signs and try to keep them awake for as long as possible, then wake them up at the change of every watch. I won't say I saved lives, but we didn't lose many."

"I didn't hit my head," Bel Ibni growled again. "I was shoved around and lost my balance, fell against a wall and grazed my face."

"That's good to know," the healer consoled Bel Ibni, then glanced across to Jacob; a shared glance between professionals. "You'll keep a watch on him?"

"Yes."

"Good. There are herbs and infusions that will ease the pain. I'll leave instructions."

Jacob watched the healer until he pushed through the ox-hide door covering, then sat on the far couch, facing Bel Ibni. "Do you want to tell me what happened?"

"No." He leaned back, and the movement made him catch his breath sharply, his face twisting in pain.

"Shoved around enough to lose your balance?"

"I was on the Processional Way. There are more people than last year. Everyone getting in everyone's way and no-one prepared to move."

"I just came along Marduk Street, Bel Ibni. There are people there, but not like the crowds of yesterday, or as large as they'll when the king arrives from Borsippa later today. You told Horam you were going to the Temple of Ishtar. There's no need to be near the Processional Way."

There was a spark of fear in Bel Ibni's dark eyes, and guilt at being caught in the lie. "Marduk Street, Processional Way. I don't remember. This is none of your concern, Jacob. Stop bothering me."

His eyes followed Jacob as the Judean stood and crossed the room to crouch before Bel Ibni. Jacob didn't want to push this, but it was time to address the rift between them.

"We've worked well together these past few years, Bel Ibni. We're an excellent team. You asked for my help with the barley you thought you'd purchased, and I was glad to help." Jacob lowered his voice and leaned forward so Bel Ibni could still hear. "There are events there I would change if I could, but I can't, and I must live with that. It's also cost me your friendship; that I can't live with and I want to change it."

Bel Ibni was silent for a moment, his eyes focused on the shrine opposite, his fingers tapping a pattern on his thigh in the rhythm he always used when he was thinking.

The Babylonian was reluctant, and Jacob couldn't work out why. Was it fear? If so, fear of what? Jacob shook his head and stood. The movement brought Bel Ibni back to the present.

"You need time to consider what I've said, Bel Ibni. We'll talk more in the next day or so. In the meantime, I have a message from Arioch. Stop trading with the Temple of Sin in Harran. Or are your injuries the same message but less subtle?"

Bel Ibni's face carried no expression. Jacob looked hard at him for a moment, then left the room.

Outside, Jacob screwed his eyes almost closed until they adjusted to the bright light. There was a hopeful look on Horam's face, and Jacob felt bad when he had to shake his head. "I made the offer, Horam. He needs some time."

"Thank you for trying," Horam said. "I'll never forget what you did for me at the Temple."

Seven moons before, Horam was accused of stealing an idol from the Temple of Marduk. The real culprit had been a small person whose head barely came to Jacob's elbow.

Now Jacob remembered the question he wanted to ask Nidintu.

"Horam. The small person who tried to blame you for the theft at the Temple. Twar, I believe they're called. Nidintu told me there were many of them in the Babylonian army at the siege of Jerusalem, and some of them returned here. Do you know if any of them are still in Babylon?"

Horam considered the question for a moment, then nodded his head. "I believe so. My father made some inquiries after the incident at the Temple. There were a dozen or more of the Twar people living in a house on Shamash Street."

"The tamkarum, Tiglath owns many of the houses on Shamash Street," Jacob said.

"My father does not believe it's a coincidence," Horam said with a nod of agreement Jacob appreciated. "Tiglath was at odds with my father before your people became a part of our business affairs. I believe Tiglath also has a following inside the Temple of Marduk."

It was Jacob's turn to nod. The Temple priests controlled all trade in and out of Babylon. Having influence or favor with them was important for every tamkarum.

"Would I be correct in believing the priests' Tiglath regards as allies do not include Arioch?" he asked.

Another nod from Horam. "If I understand correctly," the young man said. "Those allied with Tiglath are opposed to Arioch. They want his power for themselves."

It was a morning for nodding agreement and saying little. Jacob left Bel Ibni's home with much to consider. If he couldn't find the thieves who had stolen the silver and olibanum, it was very possible the plotters could unseat Arioch, or at the very least undermine his power.

That had the potential to be extremely bad for the Exiles.

CHAPTER THIRTEEN

The Babylonian New Year Festival
Day Six - Afternoon

The sun was high enough now that it dispelled the shadows in the courtyard of Isaac's home. Isaac's servants had tied bright green awnings to the posts on the upper balconies, giving welcome shade from the direct light, and adding a welcome color contrast to the sandy brown mud-brick walls. Even with the awning, the early afternoon sun was still too bright for Jacob.

Buvalu, Eli, and then Bel Ibni.

Jacob felt like he had crammed two full days into the morning. It was barely time for the midday meal but already he felt exhausted and there was a gritty itchy feeling behind his eyes.

He lounged back on a couch, closing his eyes and shielding them from the glare with his right hand. "You're getting too old for this," he muttered to himself.

"Too old for what?" Amos asked, ducking his head to come under the awning and drop onto a couch opposite Jacob. Sweat beaded his forehead, and trickled down into the white, black and brown whiskers of his beard.

"Try dragging this body around and see how you like it." He patted his ample stomach. "What are you too old for?" He asked again.

"Chasing shadows." Jacob sat forward and rested his elbows on his knees, hands in front of him, and fingers intertwined. "Ignore me, Amos. I'm just frustrated. I feel I'm missing something about this theft from Arioch. The prayer cord is too easy and too convenient. Our people can't get into the Temple that easily, and it would take a child to crawl through the shafts; they're barely a cubit wide."

"Unless it's one of the small people you mentioned. What did you call them?"

"Small people," Jacob smiled. "After Horam's experience with them, Nidintu told me who to ask about them without causing problems. They call themselves the Twar. It's the name for their home-land, supposedly near the headwaters of the Nile."

"So they're exiles like us?"

"Displaced, yes. Whether their exile was forced, or they fought voluntarily for Pharaoh, and then Nebuchadnezzar, I don't know. I'd like to speak with them but from what I've learned, they're together in a house in the New City."

Amos laughed. "There's no getting across the Adad Street bridge today. Even if you could fight your way through the crowds around the Esagila, the Temple Guards have closed the bridge until after the king returns from Borsippa."

"I know," Jacob said. "But I have to resolve this by the end of the festivities. It makes little sense, but I understand why. It's known that Arioch has valuable gifts for the Priestess of Sin."

"Is she the priestess who's close to the king?"

Jacob smiled at Amos's phrasing. "Yes, and close is an appropriate word to use. Very, very close would be more accurate. Failing to present the expected gifts puts Arioch in the position of losing face, not only with her but also with Nebuchadnezzar. He'll deflect some of that by putting the blame on us, but it will still be a blow."

"Is his position in danger?"

Jacob shrugged and thought for a moment. "I want to say no, but whoever set this up has a goal in mind. Arioch handles all the Temple's trade. It's a lucrative position with a vast amount of influence. Arioch is hard but fair. He doesn't use his position to promote favorites or to punish others, and I can think of several priests in Marduk's Temple who would do exactly that. Our merchants would be the first affected. If you think it's been difficult to get the permits and licenses for the Judah caravan, the other faction would make it impossible for us to leave the Inner City without a special permission. Permits and licenses to travel will be impossible to get."

"Can the Temple priests do that?"

Jacob smiled. For all his intelligence, sometimes the realities of the world slipped right past Amos.

"Easily. I saw similar behavior in Jerusalem. The priests gave the best trading opportunities to those who supported them, or who paid whatever the price demanded. Some merchants managed a living without being involved with the Jerusalem Temple, but it was a risky venture. It forced others out of business because they wouldn't or couldn't cooperate."

Amos's eyes had gone wide and his face paled.

Inside, Jacob wished he'd kept the words to himself, because his body remembered and his shoulders were tense and the perspiration had begun, and he could still hear the screams of those he hadn't been able to help.

"We didn't just ignore the laws Yahweh gave us," Jacob continued. "We tossed them back in his face."

It was a depressing statement, Jacob knew, and they sat for a moment with the only noise the awning flapping softly in the breeze.

"Could you cross the river north of the bridge? Have a boatman ferry you across?" Amos asked.

"We could, but the challenge is to find a sober boatman."

"If we cross over early tomorrow morning, ferry boatmen will still be sober, or at least have slept off the worst of tonight's excesses. We can check out this house you mentioned."

"We?" Jacob raised his eyebrows in apparent surprise. Inside, he felt relief.

Amos had made significant progress since reducing his wine consumption and stopping his gambling habit. He'd taken an interest in the organization and funding of future caravans. That interest had enabled preparations for the Judah caravan to keep moving forward after Nidintu, the caravan master, had disappeared.

"I'd like to come with you."

"We are going into a part of the city that belongs to Tiglath. I'm not going there looking for trouble, but it's likely to happen. Are you prepared for that?"

Amos shrugged. "I'm prepared for the trouble to happen, but I'm not so sure about being prepared to deal with it."

"There are very few people honest enough to admit that, Amos. You'll be fine if you follow my lead."

"Do you ever get nervous or scared, Jacob?"

Jacob fixed his eyes on Amos and knew the truth of his words showed on his face and in his eyes. "All the time."

CHAPTER FOURTEEN

The Babylonian New Year Festival
Day Seven - Morning

It was still early, the sun barely high enough to shine over the high city walls as Jacob and Amos made their way through the backstreets until they reached the crowds on Processional Street. The crowd jostled, bounced, and buffeted them as they joined the throng on the slow shuffle past Nebuchadnezzar's palace toward the Ishtar Gate.

The gate area itself was an enormous gap in the city walls, and all around were stacks of stone blocks waiting to be hauled into place. The crowd disturbed the construction dust, and it covered everything and everybody in a light brown haze; the dust getting into throats and noses causing a background noise of coughing and sneezing that drowned out the chatter.

Even in these early stages of construction, Jacob could see the design and picture what the finished gate would look like. He nodded in approval. This construction looked much stronger than the impressive Marduk Gate on the east side of the city, and the Ishtar Gate, once complete, promised to be stronger and even more deadly to attackers than the Marduk Gate.

This early in the day the gate guards were alert and watchful, but with so many New Year celebrants heading out of the city, unless someone drew attention to themselves the guards were content to watch and let the crush of people push their way through the gate complex. The crowd was almost treading on each other, the noise and sour smells becoming overwhelming for Jacob. He felt hemmed in, trapped. The same way as in battle. But here there was no escape, and he had no protection against a thrusting sword or a whirling mace.

Beyond the gate, and just past the northern fortress, the road branched. Most of the crowd followed the right fork, heading east toward the Temple of the New Year Festival to prepare themselves for another day of celebration. Later that day, when the king and priests arrived, there would be a lavish banquet; the first of many over the next three days.

Jacob had heard stories of these celebrations from Bel Ibni. They reminded him too much of the excesses of the elite in Jerusalem, and even feeling the way he did about his beliefs, he was glad no one expected the Judeans to take part in the festivities.

The northern road, by comparison, seemed almost empty, and Jacob pulled at the sleeve of Amos's tunic as a fit of coughing and sneezing consumed him. "Give me a minute," said as Amos paused.

"What's wrong?" The big man asked as he stopped and gave Jacob some welcome support.

Jacob let himself relax against one of the huge blocks of stone that would form part of the gate wall. He leaned forward, elbows on his knees, and head in his hands, feeling the rough edges of the stone on the back of his legs.

"Are you all right?" Amos asked again, and Jacob could hear the worry in the other man's voice.

"I will be," Jacob reassured him. "The dust and the crush of people. It reminds me too much of a battle."

He coughed again and sat back, finding himself looking directly at Amos. "Not good memories, I'd wager," Amos said.

"I've had better," Jacob admitted, and levered himself to his feet. "Come on, let's get moving again before all the boatmen get hired or drunk."

They continued on the road north, past the imposing walls of the northern fortress for another fifteen minutes before the fortress walls ended, and they came to the cluster of boatmen waiting to ferry passengers across the Euphrates.

Jacob was grateful to stay to one side, let Amos negotiate the price and a landing place on the far side of the river with a gray-haired boatman who leaned on an oar for support. His face was lined and the color of walnut, but his eyes were bright and alert. His arms, when he stood and pointed toward the boat, looked like twisted ropes of muscle.

The boat was a kelek, maybe five cubits in diameter, with animal hide stretched over a circular frame of willow branches. Jacob stepped down into the boat, wincing and shivering as the framework flexed and dipped, and chill river water slopped over his sandals, soaking his feet. He balanced awkwardly as he turned to help Amos. The big man's bulk made the small boat rock alarmingly.

"Down," the boatman barked. "Sit down, both of you, before you tip yourselves into the river."

They hurried to comply, moving in small awkward shuffles until they settled on the narrow wooden benches. Only then did the boatman step nimbly down into the boat, using the oar in his hand to unhook the line securing the boat to the shore.

As the boat drifted away from the riverbank, the boatman lowered himself to his knees and hung the oar over the side, making two powerful strokes before resting the oar in a notch behind him, and using it to guide them further out into the swift moving current of the Euphrates.

The man slit his eyes to filter the bright morning light. The sweat beading his lined forehead carried the sour, bitter scent of stale beer. A soft gust drifted the stink off the man and Jacob welcomed it, another way to disperse the dust of the crowd that still made his eyes water and his nose stream.

"Where did you say you're headed?" the boatman asked as they drifted downstream. The walls of the Southern Citadel loomed above them now, fifteen-cubits high, and with spear carrying sentries watching their progress. The high walls blocked the sun, throwing them into cooler shadow, and making Jacob shiver.

"Take us into the canal just north of Adad Street," Jacob said. "Can you let us off near Shamash Street?"

The man nodded, his long gray hair bouncing at the movement. "There are steps beyond Shamash Street." He leaned on the oar and steered the boat round an exposed mud bank. As he corrected his direction again, he gave them an assessing look. "Are you planning on staying in New City, or do you want a return trip?"

Jacob turned his head carefully, trying not to make any sudden movement that had the potential to capsize the boat and tip them into the river. He nodded toward Amos. "As he told you, we're visiting a sick relative. We won't be there all day. Maybe two or three hours."

"Pay me an additional silver piece and I'll wait for you until the middle of the afternoon. After that, you're on your own."

Jacob reached into his robe and carefully handed over the requested coin. "There'll be another one when we return to the Old City, but not if you leave us stranded."

"I value my customers, so I'll wait until an hour before sundown. After that you're on your own, because I won't risk my boat on the river in the dark."

"I understand," Jacob said, as the boat coasted gently along the canal and up to the stone platform just beyond the Shamash Street bridge. As they drifted in, the boatman pulled the oar into the boat, and stretched his arm out to steady the craft. The willow frame flexed and rubbed against the stone jetty with a soft grating sound.

"Move carefully," the boatman said. "For that extra piece of silver, I give you my word I'll be here."

Jacob smiled his thanks, turned and placed his palms on the cool stone of the jetty, then levered himself out of the boat and onto solid ground. The brief trip had cleansed his body, and he felt good again.

Once he was on the platform, Jacob leaned down and helped Amos. Again the small boat rocked dangerously and as Amos clambered out of the boat, the big man's foot slipped. Amos cursed as his shin scraped on the edge of the stone, and he ended up sprawled untidily on the dock.

The boatman turned his head away to hide a smile. Jacob focused on keeping a smile off his own face as he reached down to help Amos, but there was no need.

Amos's large frame quivered as he chuckled. "I really am too fat for this, aren't I."

Jacob kept his face neutral, then allowed the smile to come to the surface. "If you walk with the caravan to Judah, you'll slim down and by the time you return no-one will recognize you."

"Maybe. The desert trek into Exile had little effect, so I think you're being an optimist."

Amos rolled onto his left side, hunched over his legs, and pushed himself up onto his feet. He brushed the dust and grime off his robe, and smiled again at Jacob.

"Ready?"

A short flight of stone steps at the rear of the jetty took them up onto Shamash Street, where they joined the lines of people moving south to Adad Street. It was even harder to move forward as they reached the junction with Adad Street and they had to force their way across the crowds surging gently toward the bridge and the imposing walls and ziggurats of the Temple of Marduk on the opposite side of the river.

On the far side of Adad Street they were again traveling against the flow and press of revelers, and encountering resistance and surly looks as people pushed back, resenting the two of them who tried to travel against the flow.

Jacob pulled Amos off to the left and into a narrow side street.

"No sense in causing a fight," he said, rubbing carefully at his right side where one of the Babylonian men had elbowed him. "I think we'll make better time through the side streets."

"I agree," Amos said, kneading his shoulder where he'd received his own blows. "There were fingers itching to get at swords along that last section."

"Then let's not give them the satisfaction," Jacob said. He ran his left hand through his hair and stood for a moment, letting his memory bring him the layout of the new city. He pictured the pattern of streets and alleys, more organized and regular than the layout of the Old City and traced a route in his mind.

"This way," Jacob said. "If we follow this street almost to the river, we can get to the Temple of Shamash with the crowds rather than trying to go against them."

Even in the back streets, the journey was slow, and nearly an hour passed before they came to the area around the Temple of Shamash. Jacob paused at a small plaza where the regular criss-cross pattern broke down and five streets came together.

The press of people in the side streets hadn't been as bad as along the Processional Way, but Jacob put his hand on the rough serrated mud bricks of the wall of the nearest house, and leaned in for balance as he took several deep breaths. After a moment, he stood straight, and brushed the brick dust from his hands, looking around to get his bearings.

A shaft of sunlight carved along the street ahead of them, high-lighting a group of people in the middle of the plaza. Two, maybe three family groups, Jacob suspected from the combination of adults and whirling, shrieking children who dashed in and out of the group in a game that looked similar to the ones he'd seen Isaac's boys play. Two of the adults glanced up as Jacob and Amos came to the edge of the plaza. Jacob felt their dark eyes on him, assessing and judging, then flicking a cautious glance toward their children.

The two men must have decided Jacob and Amos weren't a threat, because they turned back to the group conversation. Jacob caught enough words to understand they were in the middle of a good-natured argument which of them would serve food that evening.

Jacob closed his eyes briefly, picturing the streets as he remembered them. "We want that street," he gestured to give Amos the direction. It was a narrow, empty street, dark and shadowed, and to the right of the wider avenue bright with the light of the sun.

"If Horam's correct," Jacob continued. "A street crosses this one in about a hundred and fifty paces. We go right, toward the Temple of Shamash, and it's the fourth house on the left."

"I hope for our sake Horam's memory is good," Amos said, as they made their way round the family group, careful to avoid the children who seemed oblivious to their presence.

CHAPTER FIFTEEN

The Babylonian New Year Festival
Day Seven - Morning

The street they turned into was narrower than its predecessor, barely wide enough for the two of them to walk side-by-side and avoid the trash and rotting food thrown onto the packed earth of the street. The dusty brown walls of the houses rose three storeys on each side, hiding the sun, and keeping the street in shade.

The air was still and hot, baking the fetid smells of the trash into a nauseous stink that Jacob could almost taste in the back of his throat. Like Amos, he had his arm raised, using the sleeve of his tunic to cover nose and mouth, and keep the stink to a minimum.

"Was it like this in Jerusalem?" Amos asked, as they approached the fourth house on the left.

"In Jerusalem we had wider streets, and more wind," Jacob said as he approached the door. "Even the poorer areas of the city had the wind to move the smell away."

Jacob glanced to his left and right, assessing the potential for danger from the few people on the street. A pair of urchins dressed in little more than rags squabbled over some stones. An old man shuffled along behind them in a patched and faded robe that might once have been brown, but now looked a dirty gray color.

Nothing he saw appeared to be a threat, and Jacob let himself relax a little. He'd seen worse areas in Babylon. The narrow winding streets around the Nabu Gate were dirtier, smellier, and much more dangerous.

Jacob shook the memories from his head. He'd left a man bleeding on those streets around the Nabu Gate. He had no regrets about that action but mouthed a quick and silent prayer to ask that he didn't have to do the same here. He touched his hand to his waist, checking for a sword that wasn't there, then saw the look Amos gave him.

"Old habits," Jacob explained, and turned his attention to the fourth house.

Layered panels of cured leather, so dark they were almost black, covered the doorway of the house. The skins hung from a red lintel above the door and were attached tightly to the door frame, keeping the door secured.

Jacob pushed against the leather, feeling the slick smoothness under his palm. There was no slack. The animal skins barely moved under the pressure of his hand.

"Hello. Is someone there?"

There was no response, and after a few moments, Jacob slapped his hand against the dark hide. "Is someone there?" he called. "We'd like to talk with you."

"No one in there wants to talk to you," said a harsh low voice.

Jacob turned, catching the scared look on Amos's pale face. There were four of them in a loose arc around the door. The leader stood a pace in front of his companions. He looked to be barely twenty summers old, skinny, underfed, dressed in a grubby and patched tunic and trews. His body trembled, but it was his eyes that caught

Jacob's attention: dark and glittering, anticipatory and hoping for violence.

These weren't the inexperienced Temple Guards who had assaulted Passhur, these were people who'd lived and fought in the streets probably since they could walk.

"I'm sorry," Jacob said, moving away from the doorway, nudging Amos forward as he did so. "We intended no harm. We'll leave."

"You should. You should leave now," and there was disappointment in his voice, and the slumping shoulders of his companions who had also been eager for violence.

"They're under orders not to start anything, but to react if we do," Jacob murmured at Amos as he pushed the other man back the way they'd come. He felt the four move in behind them, keeping their distance but making sure Jacob and Amos kept moving.

At the intersection, Jacob risked a glance behind him, and felt a wave of relief when he saw the thugs had disappeared. He turned his attention to Amos, whose face was pale, almost the color of mud, and his eyes were wide.

"I told you I wasn't prepared for this," Amos said between ragged breaths.

"Neither was I," Jacob admitted. "We're lucky they just wanted to scare us away. Now I'm more interested to talk to the Twar, especially if someone doesn't want is talking to them."

"They won't hear unless you talk real loud," a voice cackled. "There's no-one there. Hasn't been for two or three moons now. And that's a blessing from Marduk, I tell you."

Jacob turned and saw the old man watching them, his toothless grin mocked them. His beard was gray and straggling, too thin and wispy to trim into the traditional Babylonian spade shape. His body was bent and twisted, and his weight seemed to rest on the bamboo cane he'd placed on the ground before him.

"Why a blessing?" Jacob asked, stepping away from Amos and toward the old man.

"Because they were strange. Too strange for us," the man paused, pointed a twisted finger at Jacob, and tilted his head to one side. "From the shape of your beard, I'd say you two are some of those Judeans." He flapped his hand at Jacob, waving it to include Amos.

"No need to get offended," he continued before Jacob could say anything. "You people at least try to be part of the city. Those small people who lived here were too strange. Their food was odd. It smelled awful when they cooked, even worse when they threw out the remains. And they frightened the women and children."

"What happened?" Amos asked.

The old man shrugged. "No idea. I told you, they left two, maybe three moons ago. Whether it was their idea or Tiglath's, I don't know. Tiglath is a very successful tamkarum. He owns the building, you know. Actually, he owns most of the street, Anyway, I don't know where they went, but I'm glad they're gone. Those four you met watch the house. They won't let anyone close, and you did the right thing to walk away. They get too much enjoyment from using their knives."

Jacob felt a tingle of anticipation tickle at the hairs on the back of his neck. He'd crossed paths with Tiglath nearly a year before, and after some delicate negotiations, had extricated Amos from trouble he'd brought on himself through careless gambling and drinking. Jacob glanced across to Amos. If possible, the bigger man's face looked even paler. Amos looked like he needed to sit down. Or better yet, find the inside of a wine flask.

"My friend and I have had profitable dealings with Tiglath," Jacob said. "Do you think he knows where they went?"

"I doubt it," the old man said with a shrug. "The rumor here is those small people were only in the house because Tiglath owed someone in the Esagila a favor. When the debt was acknowledged, or paid off, Tiglath had no use for them because they paid nothing. And no one in Babylon does anything for nothing." He pointed the finger at Jacob again. "Now, you didn't hear that from me, y'understand."

"Never seen you before, or likely to again," Jacob said, with a smile the old man returned.

Jacob turned and looked at Amos as the old man shuffled past them. "The Twar were the only people who could have gone through those ventilation tunnels."

"Could they have used children? From the way you described the shafts, children could crawl through them and into the room."

"I don't think so. If we believe Arioch and Zabium, the olibanum was in sacks a child couldn't lift without help."

"Maybe someone was inside the room to help them."

"Then why not take the silver and olibanum out through the door instead of making it appear like everything went out another way?" Jacob said, unable to keep the sharp edge from his voice.

"That bothered me as well," Amos said, and Jacob was grateful the other man took no offense at his tone.

"You're as sure as you can be, that they kept the storeroom door secured?" Amos gestured at the building behind them, "and I don't mean heavy leather skins nailed in place."

"They have wooden doors," Jacob said. "When I was at the Esagila, the only calm was Arioch. Everyone else was still in panic, but I learned there's a brass lock Arioch had developed just for that door. Now, I have to understand how it works."

"How will you do that?"

"I'll tell you when I know," Jacob said. "Let's consider it while we find our boatman."

CHAPTER SIXTEEN

The Babylonian New Year Festival
Day Seven - Afternoon

The further they traveled from the house the more color came of Amos's returned to normal. The air felt cleaner and brighter. There were more people around, although families had gone from the plaza with the five streets, and Jacob wondered who had won the argument.

Instead of following their route back through the side streets, Jacob turned left to rejoin Shamash Street, just north of the Temple of Shamash.

Shamash Street was still crowded, but the press of people was less, and because they were moving in the same direction, the crowd accepted Jacob and Amos and included them in the many conversations that flowed. It took them less than a third of the time to retrace their steps to Adad Street.

As they reached the stone staircase leading down to the jetty, Jacob realized the sun had swung round and was now over his left shoulder, well into the western sky. He judged there were maybe two hours before sundown. They weren't as close to the boatman's deadline as he'd feared but reaching the Ishtar Gate before it closed for the night would be a challenge.

"Thank you for waiting," Jacob said as he helped Amos into the boat.

The boatman replied with a twisted smile. "I thought the extra piece of silver on the far side was worth the wait," he said as Jacob stepped carefully off the stone platform and took his seat.

"Besides," the boatman added, as he cast off and used his hand to push the boat away from the jetty. "I'm going to need your arms to get us back across the river to where we started." He gestured at a pair of long handled wooden paddles laying in the boat's bottom. "I hope you know how to use those. I'll need your arms to get us back across the river."

When the boat came out of the canal, the current snared them. The boat rocked and began a slow spin, traveling rapidly south toward the Adad Street Bridge.

"Get the oars, or we'll be in Erech before you know it," the boatman shouted as he drove his paddle into the water, trying to turn the boat and push them back upstream.

Jacob grabbed an oar, feeling the boat rock alarmingly as Amos leaned over and scrabbled for the other one. Water splashed over the side, soaking Jacob, and he muttered a curse as the cold shock almost made him drop the paddle. He adjusted his grip and worked the oar over the side, plunging it into the water, and mimicking the action of the boatman to move the boat upstream against the current.

"What's causing this?" Jacob asked, digging the paddle deep into the swirling water, and felt the burn of pain in his weaker right arm. Sweat trickled down his forehead and dripped into his eyes, stinging and blurring his vision.

Jacob glanced across the boat to see the boatman watching him, The man nodded approval when he saw Jacob hadn't slowed his paddling.

"One of the Armenian merchants told me it's the snow from their mountains," the boatman said. "When the snow melts in the spring, it flows into the river and the current gets faster and stronger. All that extra water trying to get to the Lower Sea as fast as it can. The river is nearly two cubits higher than usual."

"I can see the sense in that," Amos said, leaning on the side of the boat, and wheezing heavily, before using his sleeve to wipe the sweat off his forehead, and then applying himself to his task.

The boatman shrugged, and dug his paddle deep into the swirling waters, using his years of experience, and the power of his shoulders to sweep the paddle back and force them closer to the eastern shore. "Personally, I think it's Marduk's way of telling us this next year will be as hard and difficult as the last, whatever the priests tell us. Help me get across the river. The current isn't as strong under the city walls."

Gradually the three of them learned the rhythm of working together and steered the boat close to the stone walls beneath the Esagila. As the boatman had predicted, the current was weaker there, and they forced the boat back upstream, past the Southern Citadel, then the Northern Fortress, and finally back to where they'd embarked that morning.

The sun had sunk lower in the western sky by the time they'd helped drag the boat out of the river, and Jacob had handed over the promised piece of silver.

"Come on," Jacob urged Amos as they reached the road. "I want to be back in the city before the guards close the Ishtar Gate."

They hurried, Amos gasping and huffing at the additional exertion, and Jacob trying to ignore the pain in his right arm. The pain was a distraction, and not one he wanted.

"You're quiet," Amos wheezed, as they reached the first stone blocks being stored beside the road for the construction of the Ishtar Gate.

"Nothing to say," Jacob said. "We're a day closer to the deadline

Arioch gave me. He wants updates tomorrow morning, and I have nothing for him."

Jacob stopped talking as they reached the gate complex. They were nearly the last allowed back into the city. The guards watched them, and Jacob felt conspicuous in his drying clothes, crusted with the dust from the road. For a moment, he thought the guards would stop them, but they contented themselves with just watching. Although he still felt their eyes on his back, Jacob released a breath he hadn't realized he was holding.

"A moment," Amos said when they were out of sight of the guards and onto the Processional Way.

Jacob took his arm, and led Amos to the side of the avenue where they both leaned against the blue painted walls, almost black now as dusk approached.

"Even though I know I've done nothing wrong, I always feel guilty coming past any of the gate guards," Amos said, his breath still sawing in and out at a rapid rate. "Come to the house tomorrow. Isaac and Esther are leaving to visit Ezra immediately after Shema. Perhaps Miriam and I can help you find a way forward."

Jacob thought about the offer as they began walking again, avoiding small groups of people who were feeling the effects of celebrating since before noon. Jacob stepped to one side to avoid a man who lurched toward him, the beer on the man's breath like a cloud going before him.

"It won't be early," Jacob said. "I have to see Arioch before the ceremonies move to the Temple of the New Year Festival, but I will be there."

CHAPTER SEVENTEEN

The Babylonian New Year Festival
Day Seven - Evening

The sun had moved far enough into the west to put all of Isaac's courtyard into twilight shadow. Miriam moved her needles and yarn to the small table on the balcony outside her room, away from the smell of roasting meat that drifted out of the kitchen. She hoped there was enough daylight left to finish the repairs to Jacob's shawl and have it ready for Shema the following morning.

Miriam worked the needle carefully through the wool, very aware that this thinnest part of the shawl required the most care and attention. As she worked, she knew it was unlikely she'd complete the work before dusk took away the last of the light. She knew of wives and seamstresses back in Judah who regularly worked late into the night to complete repairs for the priests.

Once or twice was all right, but when it became a regular expectation, that was something else. Miriam had seen their vision destroyed by the close work and dim light. She vowed she'd never let herself be in that position, no matter how important the garment, or how much she wanted to finish the work.

As the last of the sun's light slid below the walls, Miriam laid the needle aside and, as she relaxed her concentration, the chatter of voices in the courtyard below floated up to her. She looked down and saw the soft yellow light of the oil lamps the servants had placed around the walls and on tables set for the evening meal.

Miriam heard Esther's voice, high, excited, and gushing. It was so out of character that Miriam risked standing and leaning forward slightly to get a better view.

The first thing she noticed was the table settings. The shining bronze platters suggested a special occasion almost as formal as Passover. She didn't have time to think about the meaning because Esther's voice was gushing again, and Miriam transferred her attention to her cousin who was standing, hands outstretched in welcome before Isaac and another man.

"It is an honor to have you grace our home, Priest Noah," Esther said.

His reply was an indistinct rumble, and Miriam pulled back, collecting the shawl and her tools, and retreating into her room.

Standing there, she considered for a moment changing into her best robe; the dark red one with the white needlework around the cuffs. She felt for the robe, then let the fabric slide through her fingers.

As Miriam made her way down the stairs to the courtyard, she decided she would not allow herself to be drawn into whatever scheme Esther was planning.

Esther turned at the sound of Miriam's sandals slapping on the steps. "Here's Miriam," she said in a bright voice, although in the light of the lamps, Miriam could see her cousin's eyes flash with a warning.

"I didn't know we were having guests," Miriam said, smiling at Esther. "I was so focused on the repairs to the shawl, it was only when the light went that I realized how late it is."

"No matter," Isaac said. "It's not like you're following a fool's errand into the New City like my brother, Amos."

"Don't concern yourself, Isaac. We didn't make a final decision until a few hours ago," the other man said.

He turned his attention to Miriam, and she studied him in return. His face was narrow, the bones of his cheeks prominent and hollowing out his face, sinking his dark eyes into their sockets. His skin had a pale, almost yellowish color, and Miriam guessed, if he really was a priest, as Esther had called him, he spent too many hours inside with his head bent over scrolls or clay tablets. His tan robe boasted linen of a quality Miriam hadn't seen since before the Exile.

His voice softened. "Lady Miriam, I am Noah. Isaac has told me about you, but even his praises understate your beauty."

Miriam smiled back politely, forcing herself to relax, ignore the jibe at Amos, and by extension Jacob. Noah's voice, though pleasant, had an edge to it. An edge Miriam recalled from her husband. She offered a quick prayer that her instinctive revulsion didn't make her tense up, or that her churning inside didn't betray her voice.

"You're very kind," she said. "But I suspect the light is confusing your eyes."

Another of Noah's smiles, and Miriam realized she knew how an antelope felt when pursued by a leopard. The clattering noise of the servants arriving to deliver the meal saved her from further conversation.

Miriam had been aware during the afternoon of the meat roasting in the kitchen, and although it was unusual, she had assumed Esther or the servants had found a good price on a goat. When the servants carried out the platter piled with lamb.

Miriam could barely keep the surprise off her face.

Noah's invitation to dinner was no last-minute decision.

Miriam made it through the meal. She smiled at the compliments from Esther about her needlework, and her ability to manage a household. She answered when addressed directly, and finished the small portions she'd taken for herself, even though the lamb tasted like ashes in her mouth. Better to remain silent than loose her tongue to say what it really wanted to.

When the remains of the meal were cleared away, Esther and Isaac made their excuses, supposedly to make sure the children were asleep.

"Solly is close by," Isaac said, implying the aged door guard was a suitable chaperone for Miriam.

Miriam and Noah sat in an awkward silence for a while before he finally spoke.

"I was sorry to hear of the death of your husband," Noah said. "I think we met one Passover in Jerusalem, but I also knew of him. His thinking about our laws is some of the most insightful I've heard."

"It was most unfortunate," Miriam said, her mind searching for the right words. "The journey into Exile was hard for everyone. I wish he'd shared his thoughts with me, then perhaps I could have stopped him leaving the camp that night."

"I've heard many similar stories. He was a terrible loss to the priesthood," Noah said, reaching forward for his wine, although his dark eyes never left Miriam. "Sad as it is, that is not why I'm here this evening. There comes a time when it is appropriate for a man, especially a priest, to take a bride. I want you to know I have begun discussions with Isaac about an appropriate arrangement for you to become my wife."

Although she had suspected this was the reason for Noah's visit, the actual words were like hammers into her heart. Why would Isaac allow this? Did Jacob know, and if so, had he agreed?

Miriam chose her words carefully. "You are too kind. However, I'm sure Isaac also told you I am betrothed."

Noah made a dismissive noise in the back of his throat, and his upper lip curled briefly in distaste. Another unwelcome reminder of her husband. Noah reached for the flask and refilled his wine, making no attempt to replenish Miriam's goblet, which had been empty for some time.

"It is nothing we cannot resolve. If I understand correctly, the bride price was a special arrangement as a concession to the limited means of the man involved. Our laws can only bend so far to accommodate Exile. With me, there is no question of limited means. The court has certain standards, and I will ensure you exceed them."

Despite herself, his words intrigued Miriam. "You attend King Nebuchadnezzar's court?"

He sighed, sipping at his wine again, and feigning a heavy weight of responsibility. "As a senior advisor to our Judean King Jehoiachin, it is something I must do. I have rooms in the palace itself. You will be most comfortable."

Like a caged bird, Miriam thought.

"This is not something I can answer this evening," she said. "It is much to think about and consider."

"I understand it is very sudden for you," Noah conceded. He stood, smoothing the creases from the fine linen of his robe. "Do not think too long, Miriam."

CHAPTER EIGHTEEN

The Babylonian New Year Festival
Day Eight - Morning

The central courtyard of the Esagila teemed with noise and activity. The organized chaos reminded Jacob of caravan staging grounds outside the city walls. He followed Zabium in a twisting, weaving route between braying asses and the flailing arms, cries and shouts of the priests and animal handlers as they attempted to impose order and prepare for the procession to the Temple of the New Year Festival later that morning.

Zabium was wrapped in a heavy wool cloak to ward off the early morning chill. A chill that had Jacob shivering whenever wind gusted across the courtyard. When they reached the archway leading to the inner hallways of the Esagila, Zabium paused and looked at Jacob for the first time since they two had met at the gates. Zabium's dark brown eyes were bloodshot, and there was a gray pallor on his face.

He gestured at the tall, lean officer waiting for them, and his voice was hoarse. "This is Ligish. He'll take us to Arioch."

"His Excellency is not in good humor," Ligish said in a low voice as they made their way along the hallways, threading a path between the acolytes and junior priests who hurried past on errands of their own, their robes a constant rustling that sounded like wind in the palms.

"Nothing unusual there," Zabium growled. "I hope you have good news for him, Jacob."

"Not the news he wants," Jacob said, expecting a sharp response.

Instead, Zabium merely grunted, the look on his face one of distraction. The prolonged silence made Ligish look at his Commander with concern, then glance a question at Jacob, who shrugged.

Ligish led them round a corner and up a flight of steps away from the crowds, the sound of their sandals on the stone, the only real noise. At the top of the steps, a line of men trudged past, their heads bowed as they struggled to balance the piles of mud bricks in shallow wicker baskets balanced on their shoulders.

Walking alongside the line, Buvalu the brick maker watched his workers, and used the flat of his hand to steady one, or cuff another.

"You're taking bricks out of the Temple?" Jacob said to him.

Buvalu's face twisted into a sneer of contempt. "It wouldn't be necessary if your people knew how to bake bricks properly. Replacing these is at my cost," he waved a hand toward the line of men stumbling past and aimed a slap at the nearest worker. Jacob could see the edges of each brick in the shallow basket; crumbled, flaking, and leaving a trail of gritty dust that crunched under their feet on the stone floor as they continued to a storeroom where Arioch was arguing with another priest. Temple Guards stood idly to one side engaged in their own conversations and trying not to look like they were eavesdropping, although the loud voices made it difficult not to hear.

"There's more than enough wine at the Temple of the New Year

Festival," Arioch said. "If you take any more, there won't be enough for the last feast, assuming anyone can eat or drink by then."

"Excellency."

"No!" Arioch shouted, his voice echoing back from the high ceiling, and cutting off the man's protests. "Not one more jar of wine leaves the Temple, or I will have you arrested for theft. Now leave."

The man scurried away, and Arioch turned to Zabium and Jacob.

"Well?" he demanded. "What have you learned in the last three days?"

"Not as much as you or I would like," Jacob replied. "I can tell you who wasn't involved, but little more than that."

Arioch drew in a breath, his face turning red. He looked ready to unleash his anger once more, then seemed to think better of it, and exhaled slowly. "You have two more days, Jacob. The gifting ceremony takes place after we return from the Temple of the New Year. Be sure you have answers by then."

He didn't wait for a reply, gestured at Ligish and stalked away.

"About what I expected," Jacob said to Zabium, but again the other man seemed lost in his thoughts. He nodded and waved at Jacob to begin the return journey.

As they moved back along the passageway, another soldier joined them, and Jacob recognized the guard. The man was thin, tall and arrogant. He had a look on his face that told Jacob he the incident outside Jacob's home with pleasure and had enjoyed sneaking up on Passhur's blind side.

When they reached the stairs, Jacob moved his left leg quickly, hooking his foot around the man's ankle, pushing his foot just beyond the step. The Babylonian gasped, his arms flailing as he lost his balance and pitched forward, twisting to avoid crashing his head into the stone wall, and tumbling in an awkward roll down the remaining steps, with barely time to cry out as he bounced onto the landing below, and the breath whooshed out of him.

The noisy chatter in the hallway became a stunned silence as

Jacob hurried down the steps, his sandals slapping noisily on each stone step. At the bottom, he rushed across to the fallen man.

"I apologize for my clumsiness," Jacob said loudly as he bent down and offered the man his hand to help him up. The guard struggled to his feet, wincing as the ribs he'd landed on protested. As the man came upright and their heads were close, Jacob spoke in a low voice. "If you attack one of my servants again, or any of my friends, there is nothing Zabium or Arioch can do to save you. Do you understand?"

The guard stumbled to his feet, brushed the dust off his tunic, and wiped the blood from his chin where he'd bitten his lip during the fall.

"I understand," he said with a curt nod, and turned away, the dark look on his face twisting into a forced laugh as his colleagues began chiding him for his clumsiness.

"I want you out of here before you cause more trouble," Zabium said, hooking his hand under Jacob's elbow and almost pushing him along the hallway toward the exit.

Jacob released a long sigh as he stepped outside the walls of the Esagila onto Processional Street. He leaned his back against the warm stone and let a long sigh escape from his lips. He had kept his patience with Zabium only because he sensed there was something not right. Even Ligish had looked oddly at his commander more than once.

Around Jacob, the Babylonian crowd waited in expectation. These were the faithful who wanted to be there early enough to see the god statues as they traveled to the Temple of the New Year later that day. As he moved between the groups and heard the conversation, Jacob could understand the attraction of their belief. The Babylonians offered a physical manifestation of their many gods, and there was no harm in changing allegiance from one to another. Jacob admired Bel Ibni, who kept a commitment to just one of those gods; Pasag, similar to the Judeans, who placed their faith in the one Yahweh of Abraham.

Absorbed in his own thoughts, it wasn't until a man bumped his shoulder, that Jacob realized four men in dark brown robes with hoods pulled up to hide their faces had surrounded him.

"Over there," the man on Jacob's right pointed toward one of the side streets that led to the Temple of Ishtar.

A dozen paces along the side street, there was a long stretch of wall decorated with life-size images of lions and antelopes. As Jacob passed the first animal, the four men eased behind, blocking the way back, and leaving him no option but to continue toward the thin, swarthy man in gray trews and tunic, who waited for him, with eyes slitted for protection against the bright morning sun.

"I hear you visited a house that belongs to me," he said with a hint of a smile on his narrow face as Jacob reached him. "Are you considering moving to the New City, Jacob?"

"Hello, Tiglath," Jacob said, not really surprised the man had sought him out. "I was more interested in the people who lived there, although it's a fine house."

"You mean the Twar? They left at the end of the month of Shabatu." His dark eyes studied Jacob intently for a moment. "You suspect the theft of Arioch's silver involved them?"

He chuckled at the surprise Jacob couldn't keep from showing on his face. "I make a point of knowing what's happening inside the Esagila, especially the items intended to be kept private."

"It was a possibility given their small size, but as I learned, and you've confirmed, they left the city long before the theft."

"We are well rid of them," Tiglath growled. "I hope they are back in their own land, causing their own people as much trouble as they caused me. I assume from the sour look on your face you are no closer to finding the silver than when you visited my house."

"Arioch isn't happy about it."

Tiglath gave a thin smile that made him look more like a predator than on the previous occasions their paths had crossed. "I know some of Arioch's problems," Tiglath said. "I assure you, I am not involved."

"Do you know who is?"

"Assuming I did, if I told you, it would mean my death, Jacob.

There are other priests in the Temple with a reach as long as Arioch's. I know some of what you think of me, Jacob," Tiglath said, then offered another predatory smile. "Perhaps some of it is justified. We serve different masters, and you care too much about the welfare of your people. Even the laborers who do not deserve it. I ask you tell no-one about this conversation."

Jacob looked him in the face, considered the options, then nodded. "There's nothing to tell."

CHAPTER NINETEEN

The Babylonian New Year Festival
Day Eight - Morning

There was a cool breeze drifting into the courtyard when Miriam hurried to join Isaac, Esther, and their children to say morning Shema. The wind felt cold across her face, and she shivered, pulling the woolen shawl closer around her shoulders as Isaac stood before them, lifted his arms and extended his fingers into the shape of aleph.

It was the signal for everyone to say the first words of prayer: "Hear O' Israel, the Lord is our Yahweh, the Lord is one."

The words came out of Miriam's mouth automatically. She was tired, her eyes felt sore, like they were full of sand. She shivered again because it reminded her too much of the mornings during the Exile trek from Jerusalem. She'd slept badly, tossing and turning for most of the night as she replayed Noah's visit again and again in her mind, his barely veiled suggestion he would care for her better than Jacob.

Isaac's tone shifted. Miriam grown up with the verses and could change her voice to the required and expected undertones without thinking about the changes.

As one part of Miriam's mind concentrated on the recitation, another was thinking of Jacob. It worried her he wasn't with them this morning. That, combined with Noah's visit and her most recent conversation with Esther, were like thorns in her heart.

When Isaac finished the last prayer, Miriam couldn't stop the disappointment wash over her that Jacob had not been there for the morning prayers.

As she turned away from Isaac, Esther and their children, Miriam sensed Amos come up beside her. He placed a gentle hand on her arm.

"Yesterday was a hard day for Jacob. He will be here for the midday meal after Isaac and Esther have left."

"How hard, Amos?"

He leaned in close and she could feel his breath on her cheek, warm in the cool air. "The small people, the Twar, left Babylon several moons ago. There is no way they could have stolen the silver." He stood straight, and she could see the flicker of pain on his chubby face. "On the journey back in the boat, we had to help the boatman and paddle hard to fight the river current. If we hadn't, we'd probably be down near Erech by now. Every part of my body aches, and I doubt Jacob feels any better. Worse probably, because he has nothing for Arioch who demanded to see him this morning."

"Jacob and I need to talk, Amos."

He nodded, and his sagging cheeks bounced at the movement. Amos glanced across at his brother, then back to Miriam. "I heard about your visitor yesterday. Sometimes I really don't like my family," he said, shaking his head this time. "I'll make sure you have time to talk to Jacob without interruption."

It was late in the morning before Isaac and Esther finally left the house. Without the chatter and commotion caused by the three boys, the quiet in the house made Miriam even more nervous about seeing Jacob. She attempted to distract herself by repairing a tunic Esther's eldest son had torn, but she couldn't settle, and put the fabric aside before she did more damage to the garment.

Miriam had stored the material away and was about to step out onto the second level balcony when she heard Jacob arrive. She stayed in the doorway's shadow, holding the tanned leather covering to one side so she could see without being seen, although she felt sure the men below could hear the pounding of her heart.

Jacob stood beside Solly at the entrance to the courtyard. In normal times, Jacob was maybe two or three hand spans taller than the older man. Today, his back seemed twisted and the two men looked to be the same height.

She heard Amos call Jacob's name, and when Jacob turned to greet him, Miriam could see the fatigue lining his face. Jacob moved awkwardly to greet Amos, favoring his right arm, which was clearly hurting him. Solly said something in a low voice she couldn't hear and returned to his place guarding the street door.

Miriam let the leather covering fall back into place. Four quick paces took her across the small room to the wooden chest where she kept her supply of herbs and oils. Carefully, she lifted out a phial of oil, broke the seal, and held the top under her nose. The scent was of pepper with an earthy aroma like mustard. Satisfied it was still fresh, she replaced the stopper.

Miriam realized as she looked around the room, she was delaying. She didn't want to do this, especially after seeing the pain and hurt on Jacob's face, but it was time.

She'd listened to Esther for the past two days, longer if she really thought about the way her cousin had slid innuendo and comment into nearly every conversation since the marriage to Jacob had been agreed.

Miriam deliberately scuffed her feet as she entered the courtyard, giving Amos and Jacob the chance to change their conversation. She felt Jacob's eyes on her as she approached, and met his gaze, seeing lines of fatigue and worry that hadn't been there two days ago.

She reached into the sleeve of her robe and offered the phial of oil to Jacob. "Amos told me you had a hard day yesterday. Rub this oil into your shoulder and arm. It will help the aching."

"Thank you." He took the phial, removed the top and sniffed cautiously, as Miriam had done moments before. His nose wrinkled at the peppery scent. When he looked back at her, his eyes held a question.

"It's haridra," she said. "It comes from the east, beyond Persia. The oil will warm your skin as you rub it in. Don't use too much at first because it can feel like burning."

"Probably no worse than it feels at the moment," Jacob said. "The last time I paddled a boat was on Galilee before Jerusalem came under siege."

"That's a story I'd like to hear," Amos said, and gestured toward the couches and table at the far end of the courtyard. "You can tell the story while we eat."

The food had no taste, and Miriam heard the words of the story, but missed the ending that made Amos chuckle. He refilled their wine goblets, then hefted the jug in his hand. "After that story, we need more wine," he said, and levered himself to his feet. He looked at Miriam and gave her a slight nod, telling her he was providing the opportunity he'd promised.

Miriam took a breath and a sip of the wine. She cursed herself for needing the courage of the latter, but she was afraid she was going to hurt Jacob, and that needed more than just a strong mind. If only she knew how to begin.

It was Jacob who broke the strained silence between them, leaning forward across the table toward her. "What's wrong, Miriam? Something distracted you during the meal, and I doubt you ate more than four or five mouthfuls."

"May I speak openly?" she asked in a quiet voice.

Jacob went still as he reached for his own wine. He withdrew his hand and looked her full in the face. There was a question in his brown eyes, but his voice was firm, and as quiet as hers had been.

"I've always told you there will be no secrets between us, Miriam, but I can tell something is bothering you. What is it?"

She badly wanted another sip of that wine, but pride prevented her. "Are you still committed to our marriage, Jacob? I'm told you're reluctant to set a date, and there's some question about my bride price. Isaac had a priest visit yesterday. A man who expressed his interest. If you don't want me, I will release you from any obligation." She was pleased she kept her voice calm, even though the prospect ripped at her insides.

Jacob had gone very still. His face had become like a mask that hid whatever emotions he was feeling. Very slowly, he put his hands on his knees and levered himself off the couch. There was a twist of pain on his face as he tried to move his right arm more than it liked.

She watched as he walked round the table and came to sit beside her. Miriam felt the danger in him, but oddly, she wasn't afraid.

"Did this come from Isaac?"

She shook her head, aware of how close he was, and how it distracted her. "Not directly. I suspect Esther had a hand in it."

He nodded and said something harsh in a tongue she didn't understand.

"Armenian," he explained, and then with a soft smile that brightened his face, and smoothed away the lines. "No, I won't translate it for you."

For a moment, Jacob seemed uncertain whether to sit forward or retreat, then he moved forward and pulled Miriam's hands into his own. His grip was firm, and his calloused fingers were warm in her palms.

"I delivered your bride price to Ezra the day after Isaac and I agreed the terms. I have been asking Isaac to confirm a date for nearly two moons, but every time he delays with one excuse or another. I don't know Esther's motives."

Only then did his shell crack a little, and it was the brief hesitation in his voice that gave Miriam the insight.

"I've told you before how my marriage was arranged to build an alliance between our families. Neither of us had any say in the decision. When she died in childbirth, it was a release for both of us."

His brown eyes fixed on Miriam, and she felt she could see into his soul, and feel the warring emotions of relief and guilt. They were feelings she knew well from her own marriage and widowhood.

"I decided that day, should I ever marry again, it would be because of how I feel about the person, and not for any other reason. I know, you're the woman I want, Miriam, and I hope you feel the same way."

CHAPTER TWENTY

The Babylonian New Year Festival
Day Eight - Afternoon

Jacob felt the wine churn in his stomach as he waited for Miriam to respond to his last words. The conversation, although not unexpected, had caught him by surprise, although he should have guessed Isaac wasn't being truly honest with him.

The awkward silence between them returned, and as Jacob realized Miriam hadn't answered his question, he felt the churn slide deeper into his guts. He'd thought he was on certain ground after what she'd said, but it seemed he'd misunderstood her words.

There was a stricken, almost horrified look on her face. It was a look Jacob knew would haunt him for a long time. Carefully, he eased away from her, noting the shimmer of tears in her eyes. He struggled for words. Any words, but his mind refused to provide them.

A noise from the far side of the courtyard saved him.

He looked up and saw Solly with Huba, Bel Ibni's door guard.

The two of them were about the same age, stooped over, the brown skin on their arms and faces blotched with the marks of age. And so alike they could be brothers.

"Passhur told me you'd be here, Jacob," Huba said in his high-pitched voice that sounded like the wind rustling through the marsh grasses. "I have a message for you, and for the lady Miriam. Bel Ibni asks you to join him as soon as it is convenient for you."

Jacob looked at Miriam, and she gave a shrug. "Now is as good a time as any other," and then to the two older men. "Give us a minute. We'll join you outside."

Jacob clenched his jaw as she moved close to him, her warm woman scent a heady aroma as he breathed deeply, trying to remain focused.

"You know my family are Levites, and my husband was also a priest. My family, and most especially the men, are never open about their feelings. When you say the things you do, Jacob, it's like hearing the Babylonians speak faster than I can understand. It takes a while for me to catch up."

She pressed close then, molding her body to his, flooding him with her scent, and he could barely hear her low voice above the pounding of his heart. "I'm not giving you up, Jacob. Not today, not tomorrow, and not next year. A few moons ago, you suggested we leave Babylon and go to Sippar or Erech. I'm ready to do that if you are."

Jacob hooked his good left arm around her waist as the fear and anger and tension washed away from him. "Let's deal with Bel Ibni, then you and I can finish this conversation properly."

"Let me get my herbs and oils," she said, the reluctance to leave his embrace clear in her voice.

Bel Ibni lay propped on the same couch he'd used when Jacob visited two days before. Instead of being inside the house, the couch sat under a red awning that provided much needed shade and color to the courtyard. There was a low table before the couch, a chair and another couch arranged around the table.

Horam sat in the chair, conversing with his father in a low tone. They both looked up when Huba announced Jacob and Miriam, and Horam bounced to his feet as Huba retreated into the shadows with Solly.

He came toward them with a nervous smile that made his thin face look more pointed and angular.

Behind Horam, Bel Ibni eased himself carefully into a more upright position on the couch. Bel Ibni was too far away, and his face masked by the shadows of the awning for Jacob to read the man's expression, but the involuntary jerk of the Babylonian's head as he moved, told Jacob Bel Ibni was still in pain.

"I wasn't sure you'd come," Horam said as he reached them.

"Was Huba's message from you or your father?" Jacob asked as he gripped Horam's hand in greeting.

"It was from him, although I may have had a hand in crafting the words," Horam said with a smile as he led them toward the couches under the awning and out of the sun's glare.

Flaunting convention, Miriam sat on the second couch with Jacob, close enough that he could feel the warmth of her thigh beside his. From the corner of his eye, Jacob thought he saw a smile on Horam's face, but he remained focused on Bel Ibni.

The Babylonian still favored his left arm, and the bruises on his face looked softer and less colorful than they had the day before. Bel Ibni leaned forward carefully, and offered a bronze plate of dates to Miriam, then Jacob.

"I asked you both to come for similar reasons," Bel Ibni said as he replaced the plate on the table between them. "I hope that after we've talked, you will honor me by breaking bread once more at my table. I'm not seeing much joy in this new year. Hopefully, we can make it so the coming year is better for all of us."

"I also hope that's where our talk leads," Jacob said. "Where should we begin?"

"With your approval, I will talk with Miriam first," Bel Ibni answered. Bel Ibni turned his attention to Miriam, and again there was the slightest wince of pain on his face as he moved. "I have said it many times, Miriam, that you have some of the best healing abilities in the city. When I needed a healer, instead of asking for you, I insisted on someone I barely know. An amateur who knew less than Jacob. Horam and my wife, Erau, haven't let me forget it."

"I can look at your injuries before we leave," Miriam offered. "There are salves I can give you to help with the pain you're suffering from the bruises."

"Thank you," Bel Ibni smiled, then lifted his gaze to look directly at Jacob. "We have different, and deeper issues, Jacob. You have been a good steward of my trading business these past years. You have the mind and an enthusiasm I no longer have. I've been trying to develop other areas of business and neglected what has given me a good life."

For a moment, Jacob wanted to throw it all back at Bel Ibni, use the Babylonian's own words back at him and let the anger he'd suppressed all this time fuel his words. Then he sensed Miriam's quick and worried glance at him, felt her tense beside him, and realized how well she knew his moods.

Jacob took a long, slow breath before answering. "You should have talked to me, Bel Ibni. And I should not have been so stiff-necked. Is it trading the barley crops that excites you now, or something else? Something that doesn't require haggling with unreasonable tamkarum and priests?"

"Something else," Bel Ibni admitted. "I've had a lot of time to think these past days. I feel everyone I deal with wants something for nothing, or even less. This will be my fortieth New Year celebration. The back and forth and the negotiations that used to excite me now frustrate me. I'm tired of it, and I want to enjoy my time with Erau and the grandsons Horam will give us."

"Let me get married first, father," Horam said with an equal mix of laughter and embarrassment.

"What are you suggesting?" Jacob asked.

"Today, you probably know my business better than I do, and you've been a good steward. Your thinking differs from the traditional

Babylonian way of doing things. Going to Nineveh, for example. Most of the people in this city have forgotten it ever existed, but you want to trade with them. That's why I want you to become a partner and teach Horam what you know."

"I can't keep him too busy," Jacob said. "Or he won't have time to deliver those grandchildren you want."

"I'll make it worth your while," Bel Ibni said. "We can discuss it in more detail if you'll have wine with me and stay for the evening meal."

Jacob looked over at Miriam, and saw the thoughtful look on her face, the slight frown that creased her forehead when she was thinking. "It could be a good idea," she breathed.

"I must send Solly to Amos," Jacob said. "So he and Isaac do not worry about Miriam. Then I think wine is an excellent idea."

While Jacob gave Solly the message for Amos, the servants brought out wine and goblets, and Miriam inspected Bel Ibni's injuries.

She had pushed the sleeves of her robe above her elbows, giving her arms freedom of movement as she used her hands to trace the wounds.

"It's mostly bruising and a few scrapes," she said finally, stepping back and letting the sleeves fall down to her wrists. "Your breathing sounds good, so I don't think it's anything more serious. Rest for another day, two if you can." She reached into the small basket she'd brought with her, her fingers hovering over the contents until she selected two small clay jars.

"These contain a vinegar made with apples. Rub it into your bruises at night, and in the morning. It will help with the pain and swelling."

"Thank you." Bel Ibni's fingers closed around the jars and he placed them on the table before him, using the opportunity to lift one of the wine goblets.

"This is the last of the wine from the Armenians," he said with a sigh.

Jacob nodded sympathetically as sipped at the wine. His own stock of Armenian wine was equally depleted. He expected the usual faint taste of fig and plum. Instead, the flavor of the dry wine came alive on his tongue as he swallowed. There was a delicate taste of plum, and something else. Not fig.

"Olives?" he asked.

For the first time in too long, Bel Ibni smiled, and there was genuine humor and amusement in his dark eyes. He nodded. "Olives, and pomegranate. It comes from the Arpa river. The Armenian merchant told me they've been supplying wine since the time of the first Nebuchadnezzar." He smiled again. "I'm not sure I believe that, but the wine's good."

"It is once you get used to the flavor," Jacob agreed, setting his goblet down, and choosing his words carefully.

"Bel Ibni, if you want me to teach Horam everything, I need to know about your trading with the Temple of Sin in Harran," Jacob said. "When did you begin trading with them?"

Bel Ibni frowned and chewed at his upper lip. "Three, maybe four moons ago. They wanted linens, so I sent some, and it's grown from there."

"They approached you?" Jacob couldn't keep the surprise from his voice.

"Yes. I know Arioch regards that trade as exclusive to the Temple of Marduk. Or exclusive to Arioch himself. The people I spoke with led me to believe Arioch had given his blessing, that the linens we can provide are better than his."

"Arioch will never admit his goods are inferior," Jacob said, and both men smiled. "He still regards trading with the Temple of Sin as his exclusive right. He made it very clear to me yesterday that your trading must stop."

"You're sure the people you met represented the Temple of Sin?" Miriam said, taking another small sip of wine. Jacob could tell from the slight crinkling of the fine lines around her eyes she didn't care for the taste and was being polite.

"Of course, I'm sure," Bel Ibni said, some of the usual sharpness coming into his tone. "They were with the Priestess at the last New Year Festival. That was when we first spoke, although it took a long time to arrange ethe first shipment."

Jacob placed his goblet on the low table, sitting back and shaking his head as Bel Ibni made to refill the goblet. He tugged at his beard as he thought, smoothing the shape back into a point with his fingers.

"I doubt Arioch was behind the attack on you. My guess is it's whoever is behind the attempt to undermine Arioch's position within the Esagila." Quickly he told Bel Ibni and Horam about the theft of the silver and olibanum.

"Were you able to learn anything useful from the Twar?" Horam asked.

Jacob shook his head. "They left the house two or three moons ago. It's possible there are some still in the city, but I doubt it. I told Amos yesterday evening, I need to know more about the lock, but Arioch is at the Temple of the New Year Festival for another two days, and I can't get to him."

"This lock maker. Is he Egyptian?" Bel Ibni asked, refilling his own goblet, and passing the jug to Horam.

"I believe so."

"Then I can help," Bel Ibni said. "His name is Aatami, which means man, although I'm told he had another name before he left Egypt. He has a workshop on the far side of the Enlil Gate near the Outer Wall. Horam did not like him."

"Is that the man who was here to secure your business room?" Horam asked, getting to his feet as the servants appeared in the courtyard carrying platters of food.

Bel Ibni nodded, and Horam directed a sympathetic smile toward Jacob. "Aatami may be brilliant, but I wish you well, Jacob. He makes the worst of my father look like a placid child. How someone so small can have so much arrogance, I have no idea."

Jacob couldn't keep the smile off his face as he glanced up at the red awning, gauging the sun's position in the sky. There were still several hours of daylight remaining.

"You want to go now, don't you," Miriam said.

When Jacob looked at her, she had a smile on her face, and he wondered again how she knew him so well.

"I'll wait here," she said. "However long it takes."

"Go where? Oh. The lock maker," Bel Ibni said, as he too glanced at the sky. "He still uses the Egyptian way of counting the days, so New Year for him is still some moons away. I can almost guarantee Aatami is working today. I'll give you directions. If you leave now, you can return in time for the evening meal, and I'll see if perhaps we have one last jug of the Armenian wine."

"If I'm not here, eat without me," Jacob said. "I don't know how long this will take."

CHAPTER TWENTY-ONE

The Babylonian New Year Festival
Day Eight - Afternoon

The streets were quieter than Jacob had seen them in the past seven days. After living in Babylon for four years, he knew there was a point when the celebrations and reveling paused, and it seemed to be when the priests and nobles of the city left for three days of their own celebrations at the Temple of the New Year Festival.

The public celebrations would begin again in three days when the statues of the Babylonian gods returned to the Esagila. After one final and extravagant banquet, the Temple of Marduk would return the god Nabu to Borsippa, and Babylon could return to normal.

Meanwhile, Jacob was grateful he could travel through the city with none of the crushing and pressing crowds he'd fought against for the past three days. He walked quickly, but cautiously. The ease with which Tiglath and his men had come upon him, still disturbed Jacob. He'd allowed himself to forget many things from Jerusalem. Things he needed to remember if he was going to match wits with Tiglath and maintain his claim on Miriam.

The guards at the Enlil Gate huddled inside the gate house out of the sun, and with little enthusiasm to give any traveler more than a cursory glance. Jacob saw they had a flagon of wine, and reliance on the security provided by the Outer Wall. It was a laziness that would have demanded punishment when he'd been a solider in Jerusalem, because Judah's wars had always been close to home, not like the Babylonians who marched for days, or weeks to find an opponent in battle.

Jacob shook his head as he came to the far side of the gate, crossed the canal, and turned to his left, following the directions Bel Ibni had given him. On his left side was the canal, the brown water moving sluggishly along toward the main flow of the Euphrates, the energy of the water lost in the huge loop the canal made around the Inner Wall of Babylon.

On Jacob's right, there were patches of scrub, with grazing goats tethered to stakes. The animals looked up as Jacob passed, their eyes following him, and protested his presence with the occasional bleat. At the first group of mud-brick buildings, Jacob turned away from the canal and into a wide street with two and three-story buildings.

Jacob had spent most of the four years of Exile in the north-east of the city where the caravans assembled. He rarely came here, to these deserted streets. The late afternoon sun burned at him off the mud-brick walls. He walked the two stadia Bel Ibni had told him, then turned into another street and lifted a hand to protect his eyes from the glare of the reflected sun.

Inside the inner walls of the city, the bricklayers applied their artistic talent to carve and shape the exterior of the mud bricks into a series of sharp decorative ridges that cast shadows across the wall. The ridges broke up the monotony of the walls into elegant and elaborate shadow patterns, and reduced the glare of the sun.

Here, where the buildings rose two or three storeys high, with the brick surfaces flat, smooth and bouncing back the glare of the sun with such intensity, Jacob had to screw his eyes almost closed.

These were the workshops of artisans; woodworkers and metal-workers, mostly. The workshop of Aatami the Egyptian looked no different to any of the others along the quiet street. The stink of refuse, so prevalent in the rest of Babylon, was missing here, where the residents kept the streets clean. There was still a familiar sour odor in the air. The smell was out of place here, and Jacob couldn't put a name to it.

The street made a long shallow curve to the right, back toward the ramparts of the Outer Wall. It was quiet except for the chatter and buzz of the insects and other bugs. If he concentrated on listening, Jacob could hear the low murmur of noise from the crowds around the Esagila.

The workshop Jacob sought had a door made from panels of cedar instead of the more traditional layering of animal hides. The polished panels shone in the sunlight, adding to the glare from the walls. Jacob noted the red lintel above the door, and wondered if the traditional Babylonian ward against evil spirits was something Aatami believed in as well, or if it was a concession to his workers.

There was no noise from within the workshop. Jacob lifted his hand to rap his knuckles on the wood and heard a noise from the direction of the Outer Wall. Looking that way, he saw the long shadow of a man approaching. Jacob felt for the knife strapped to his right forearm wishing he carried a sword, or better still, there was somewhere for him to step out of sight.

Jacob moved away from the door to give himself room as the shadow twisted and turned and a man came into view. He felt a combination of relief and frustration as he recognized the man.

"What are you doing here?" Zabium came to a halt before Jacob, his bull-like head jutting forward, one hand resting on the hilt of the sword strapped to his waist.

"Probably the same as you," Jacob said, noting the Babylonian's haggard look and bloodshot eyes. Zabium looked worse than he had at the Esagila the previous day. Jacob considered challenging him about it, then focused on the current challenge.

"There are only two ways into that storeroom. The shafts, or the door. If the silver and olibanum weren't taken out through the shafts, then however unlikely it seems, they went through the door."

"Arioch has the only key."

"Arioch has the only key you know about," Jacob said. "Aatami must have some way of recreating the lock, and the key if he needs to. Unless you think he stole the silver and olibanum."

Zabium laughed, a deep rumble from his belly that showed actual humor for the first time. "Unlikely. He's shorter than most of the acolytes at the Temple, with arms and legs like sticks, both too long for his body. He barely has the strength to carry his own tools. I doubt Aatami could lift one of the silver crates, let alone all ten."

Despite his concern at Zabium's too convenient appearance, Jacob smiled at the image Zabium had drawn of the Egyptian lock-smith. "Let's find out if he has the strength to open his own door."

When Jacob's knuckles rapped on the polished cedar panels of the door, the door swung partly open. The smell Jacob had noticed earlier was stronger now, and mixed with the tang of smoke.

A smell he could now put a name to.

As the door swung further open, Jacob reached into the sleeve of his robe, pulling the knife free from its strapping on his right forearm.

"Something's wrong," he said to Zabium and stepped through the doorway toward the smell.

Through the door, Jacob found himself in a dimly lit passageway the width of four men walking abreast. The air was warm and stale and carried the same smell toward him from the far end. There were darker rectangles at intervals that Jacob guessed were entries to rooms.

As he continued forward, he heard the scuff of Zabium's sandals on the stone floor behind him. "You check the right-hand side. I'll work the rooms on the left," the Babylonian said in a whisper that barely carried to Jacob.

Jacob lifted his right hand in acknowledgement, realizing Zabium had remembered Jacob was left-handed, and giving him the side of the passageway that would be an initial advantage in a fight. Jacob paused at the first doorway. There was no sound from inside the room. He shifted the knife in his hand as he risked a brief glance.

In the half-light Jacob saw a bench with some unfamiliar looking tools scattered across the surface, and a small mound of something that looked like yellow colored earth. There was no-one there, or in any of the others.

An animal hide covered the last door at the end of the hallway. The hide was stiff and heavy. Jacob had to switch the knife to his right hand, using the strength in his left arm to get the leverage he needed to pull the skin to one side. Jacob screwed his eyes into a squint as bright sunlight flooded into the hallway, along with a wave of the smell that had been getting progressively stronger.

"Over here, Zabium," he said, and when the Babylonian joined him, Jacob pointed out into the courtyard. Most of the courtyard was in shadow, but there was enough light to see the dark puddle of blood that had congealed around the head of the man sprawled face-down on the ground with the legs bent and the long bony arms flung forward. The direction of the body was away from a construction that looked like a kiln. The sour rotting odor had blossomed as Jacob had pulled back the hide. Flies swarmed around the pool of dried blood, their buzzing unnaturally loud, and to Jacob, disrespectful.

Jacob took an involuntary step back as the rotting stench rose so strong, he could almost taste it in his throat. He turned away and retched, not sure if he was glad to keep down the fruit and nuts he'd eaten at the midday meal, feeling the bitterness of the Armenian wine rise from his stomach and burn the back of his throat.

He turned away from the body, took a series of deep breaths, swallowed hard, then looked across at Zabium, whose normally tanned face looked gray and haggard.

"I assume that's Aatami," Jacob said, gesturing at the scrawny body with thin, stick-like arms and legs, exactly as Zabium had described him. Jacob slid the knife back into the sheath strapped to his right forearm. That done, he transferred his attention to the kiln structure on the far side of Aatami's mangled corpse.

The structure stood slightly higher than Jacob's head, and about a cubit wider than Jacob's outstretched arms. It was constructed with clay bricks, and the side nearest to Aatami had blown out, leaving rock debris and dust all over the ground. Thin trails of gray smoke drifted out of the hole, bringing with it the faint odor of garlic, and an intense heat. The heat brought beads of sweat to Jacob's forehead as he studied the debris on the ground before him. There were twisted and misshapen pieces of metal among the rock fragments. Jacob selected a piece and picked up it up carefully. The metal, bronze he guessed from the reddish color, was still warm to the touch.

"What was Aatami doing?" Jacob asked aloud, although he was really talking to himself.

"He told Arioch he was going to build his own foundry to shape and form the metal so he didn't have to spend so much time traveling to the foundries in Borsippa." Zabium paused as he reached Jacob's side. "Do you smell garlic?"

Jacob nodded. Zabium stepped a handful of paces back and away from the shattered kiln, pulling Jacob with him.

"He was using arsenic as part of his smelting process. Breathe carefully around the kiln or you could end up poisoned, and have dark patches all over your skin," he pointed at the marks where the explosion had ripped away Aatami's robe and exposed his back.

"How do you know this?"

"One of my jobs in the Army was to check the quality of the swords and spears we bought. To do that, I learned the smelting process and gained two impressive burn scars."

"Wouldn't it have been easier for Aatami to remain in Borsippa, or work with the smiths in Kweiresh rather than expose himself to these dangers?"

"For you or me, probably," Zabium agreed. "Aatami prided

himself on being the only lock maker in Babylon. It's difficult to say that when you live in Borsippa."

Jacob let himself smile at the words, wondering why Zabium had ignored the option of Kweiresh. He considered challenging the man, but let it go for the moment. Instead, he said. "Aatami must have been a man with powerful beliefs about his own abilities."

"Very much so. He was always ready to tell you how much superior his skills were. I don't think Arioch liked him very much as a person. I know I didn't, but he was an excellent craftsman. Are you finished here? I want soldiers from the Outer Gate to clean this up and give Aatami the funeral rites."

"I haven't begun, Zabium. I came here to learn about Aatami's locks and keys. I still want that knowledge."

"He's dead."

"Very convenient for the people who stole from Arioch," Jacob said. "I'm going to spend time here looking for anything that might help find who took the silver and olibanum. I didn't need you before, I don't need you now, Zabium. You can help, or you can wait until I'm finished."

Jacob was watching Zabium closely, and he knew he'd have missed the man's reaction otherwise. There was a flash of fear on the Babylonian's face, then anger, and a deliberate effort to be calm.

Jacob understood the last two, but the first emotion surprised him. Why was Zabium afraid? And of what?

"Tell me what you're looking for, and I'll help," Zabium said after a deep breath. "Aatami won't resent being left for another hour or two."

"I'm looking for scrolls or tablets. Anything to show how he built the Temple lock. Aatami must have kept something. If Arioch lost or broke the key, there must have been a way to replace it."

Zabium sighed and looked around at the debris. "Where do we begin?"

CHAPTER TWENTY-TWO

The Babylonian New Year Festival
Day Eight - Evening

The last flickers of daylight had disappeared when Jacob arrived back at Bel Ibni's home. The red awning had been replaced with oil lamps that cast a yellowish glow, bringing with it the nutty smell of burning sesame. Although he much preferred the lamps of Judah that used olive oil and gave off a sweeter scent, Jacob breathed the nutty odor with relief.

He and Zabium spent the rest of the afternoon searching Aatami's workshop with no success. They had found several heaps of smashed and crushed clay tablets, and a pile of cold ashes that Jacob was certain had once been papyrus scrolls. If Aatami had plans of the lock he'd made for Arioch, they were no longer in the workshop.

"Your look says it was not a successful expedition," Horam said, coming to Jacob and offering him wine. "It's not the Armenian wine my father is so pleased with," he said, seeing Jacob's hesitation.

Jacob smiled his thanks, but still shook his head, declining the offer. He pulled his slumped shoulders back, straightened his back and across the courtyard saw Miriam and Bel Ibni watching him. To their left, almost hidden in the shadows, Amos.

"He's worried about you," Horam said, following Jacob's gaze. "I think you have a solid ally there."

"Amos is a good man," Jacob answered. "It's taken him longer than many to adjust to our Exile. The Judah caravan has given him a purpose again. And he's protective of Miriam."

"A past rival?"

Jacob shook his head. "His wife died of fever during the siege of Jerusalem. I think the caravan will give him the chance to visit her burial place and maybe put her memory to rest."

"My bride, Damkina, has a sister."

Horam laughed loud at the sharp glance Jacob gave him. Jacob chuckled as well. The release of his own tension was welcome, and he patted Horam on the arm.

"That conversation will require a different evening, and a lot of wine." Jacob gestured toward the others, looking over at them, and intrigued by the humor. "Let's join them, so I only need tell the story one time."

Once he'd told everyone what had happened at Aatami's, Jacob was ready to leave.

There were few people on the streets, although they could hear the buzz of celebration from the Esagila to the west. The smell of cooking fires drifted over them, and Jacob felt his belly rumble with hunger. It had been many hours since he'd eaten. Even though the streets looked safe, Jacob had Miriam walk between Amos and himself.

They were barely a hundred paces away from Bel Ibni's house, when Miriam broke the silence between them.

"Can I ask what the two of you have been doing these past weeks? You, especially Amos, have been like the boys when they find something new to amuse them."

"You know I've been helping Ezra's scribes document our tradition?" Amos said.

"I hear there have been quite some arguments," Miriam said in an amused tone. Her ability to see humor in any situation was one of the many things Jacob liked about her.

"I've heard it's one continual argument," Jacob said. "Besides documenting our tradition, Amos is taking to all the soldiers he can find who will talk with him. The idea is it will help our leaders in the future after we return from Exile. He seems to think I can help."

"Think?" Amos said. "I get more sense in an afternoon with you, than I do after days with our priests. I know it's late, and your day has been frustrating and long, but if you could give me some time this evening, it will help keep Ezra's impatience in check."

Jacob suppressed the sigh that rose in his throat. Amos was right, it had been a long day, and he was tired. His right arm was still sore from the exertions of the previous day and the lifting he'd done at Aatami's foundry.

What he really wanted was the solitude of his own home, where he could apply the oil Miriam had given him, and think about what had happened. Think about it and decide what to do next. There were two days before Arioch presented the gifts of silver and olibanum to the Priestess of Sin, and he had no ideas.

"If it helps," Miriam said as they turned the final corner and came to the door of Isaac's home. "I can massage the haridra oil into your shoulder while you talk to Amos. If you don't mind me hearing about your past."

Jacob let his mind drift to the pleasant thought of her fingers massaging his shoulder and arm.

"Some of it will be ugly, and some of it makes me look a fool," he said. "However, I would welcome the relief from the oil, and your hands." He turned and looked at Amos across the top of Miriam's head. "Remind me what we last spoke about, Amos."

After a long pause, Amos said. "If I can remember what I wrote, and assuming I heard it correctly, you were talking about understanding your enemy. Once you have that understanding, you can plan your strategy. Whether the strategy is attack or defense, you can drive your opponent the way you want him to go."

Jacob halted in mid-stride. "Say that again."

Amos repeated his words, and realizing Jacob was no longer with them, he too paused, and put his hand on Miriam's arm to stop her.

"What is it?" Amos asked.

"They know me," Jacob said, the realization coming to him with the power of a blow to the head. "Whoever is behind this guessed Arioch would contact me, or made certain he would. They know about the theft of the statue involving Horam and the Twar. They left just enough crumbs to be certain I'd follow the path they wanted me to." He rolled his head back toward the dark sky and closed his eyes. "How could I have been so blind?"

"You're not making any sense, Jacob. I don't understand."

Jacob opened his eyes and smiled at the confusion on Amos' face, and the concern in Miriam's dark eyes. "Don't worry, Amos. I don't expect you to understand. You haven't seen or heard everything I have, and I still missed the most important points."

"We are nearly at the house," Miriam said. "It's just the three of us. Amos came to tell me Isaac and Esther are staying with Ezra this evening."

Inside the house, Jacob sat on the hard wooden couch at the end of the courtyard farthest from the door. As he listened to the noises of Amos lighting lamps, and Miriam talking with the servants in their quarters, he carefully lifted his right arm as far as he could, and moved it in small circles. The movement was a combination of pain and pleasure.

Jacob focused on the exercise, and was ready to push himself harder, when he felt a firm and smooth hand on his wrist.

"Enough," Miriam said. "You'll make it worse if you don't take proper care of that arm."

Gently, she pushed his arm down, angling it so his hand was on his left shoulder. Jacob gasped a little when her hand slid under his robe and her fingers, slick and cold with the haridra oil touched his skin.

"It will warm up in a moment," she said.

The warmth came quickly. As the warmth flooded across his shoulder, Jacob felt himself relax, and the thought that had eluded him from the start presented itself to him.

"There's one important thing I don't know," he said. "Is this a plot aimed at us Exiles, or at Arioch."

Amos sat opposite Jacob with a tablet and stylus in his hands. He tilted his head to one side and stopped, twirling the stylus between his fingers. "Had you considered it might be both?"

"I have, and that means the fortune of every Exile in Babylon is dependent on Arioch remaining where he is."

Amos stopped twirling the stylus between his fingers. Miriam's hands slowed their massage, and in the silence, Jacob saw a way forward.

"I have to go to Kweiresh."

"Why Kweiresh?" Miriam asked, her fingers tightening on his shoulder.

Jacob moved his shoulders. Miriam stopped her gentle massage and trailed her fingers across his neck as she withdrew her hands. Jacob shivered and stood. He hoped being active would bring more clarity to his decision.

That, and some distance from Miriam.

Jacob paced the length of the courtyard and then back to the couches. As he walked, he eased his arm from one side to the other. There was no ache, and his shoulder felt better than it had in a long time.

"I don't know, Miriam, but every time I think I come closer to understanding this puzzle, Kweiresh is mentioned and I reach a dead end," he turned back to look at Miriam and Amos, using his fingers to count each point he was making.

"Samuel believes the blue cord comes from Kweiresh. The Judeans at the brickworks are from Kweiresh. Aatami could have built a proper foundry for his locks and keys at Kweiresh, using the expertise of the people there, but he tried to construct his own foundry in the south of the city. Tiglath made a comment about my misplaced concern for the laborers. Kweiresh is where they live."

Amos made some marks on the clay tablet and put his stylus to one side. "Had you considered it might be coincidence?" he asked. "Or that Arioch arranged it?"

"Nothing about this has been a coincidence," Jacob said. "I've considered Arioch as the person behind the theft, but it makes little sense. He lives well and has a large family. The amount of silver wouldn't last him a half-year, even if he could hide from the Temple."

Jacob reached for the flagon of wine, then thought better of it. "Am I being pushed toward Kweiresh, and if so, why? What's there?"

"It's a rough area," Amos said. "If these people believe you're making progress, Kweiresh would be a good place to lure you. When I was gambling, there were several men who owed money to the lenders. Those invited to a meeting in Kweiresh never returned."

"You should not go, Jacob."

Jacob saw the fear in Miriam's brown eyes and felt some of it himself. It wasn't the unknown; he had conquered that demon many years before. It was the feeling he was being herded and driven like an unsuspecting sheep.

Driven to the slaughter.

Jacob reached across the low table, picked a date from the platter and chewed on it. He took Miriam's hand in his.

"I still don't know what I'm looking for. It could be as much a wasted day as our attempt to find the Twar. Or, as you fear, a trap. Either way, I have to go."

CHAPTER TWENTY-THREE

The Babylonian New Year Festival
Day Nine - Morning

After his experiences at the Ishtar Gate two days before, Jacob made
the longer journey to Kweiresh. It meant using the Marduk Gate and
then walking almost three sides of a square to the north of the city, to
where Kweiresh was situated midway between the Ishtar Gate and
the Summer Palace.

There had been the expected crowd of revelers nursing hang-
overs at the Marduk Gate, and many more than the few he'd seen
with Zabium the morning they visited the brickworks. Under the
watchful eyes of the gate guards, the revelers caused no trouble,
although Jacob considered the reek of stale beer and wine, its own
offense.

Away from the gate, with fewer people and clearer air to breathe,
Jacob turned north, following the track that led alongside the canal
until both track and canal turned west. At that point, Jacob could see

the smoke haze from the foundries hanging over Kweiresh. His slow trudge eased to a stop.

It was time to decide.

Jacob needed a reason to be in Kweiresh. A credible reason, so he wouldn't be immediately suspect if the thieves were there and recognized him. He'd spent most of the night, and all the journey so far, trying to think of a reason but with little success.

"Like beating my head against a wall," Jacob growled to himself, and then Bel Ibni's words echoed in his head. *I should get a proper door for this room, then you can beat your head against it.*

"I need a door. A metal door for my house," Jacob said aloud. The tension eased out of him, and while the feeling of relaxation wasn't as intense as when Miriam had massaged his shoulder the previous evening, he still felt good.

As he continued walking, Jacob for the first time took notice of the surrounding land. It was like the area near Samuel's home: clusters of houses, each larger than his own inside the city walls, the bleating of goats, and the occasional deeper tone of a sheep.

The canal he was walking alongside served as a major irrigation source for the gardens and crops that stretched away north and east toward the outer walls of the city. Ahead and to the right were the imposing towers of the Summer Palace, the sand-colored ramparts supposedly the remaining foundations of the great tower of Babel, built when this land was called Shinar.

There was space here, Jacob realized. Space to live and maybe raise children. He hadn't considered it before, hadn't discussed it with Miriam, but the idea appealed to him.

It was late morning when the fields slowly began giving way to buildings: initially stables, and then on both sides of the track, small, poorly built and badly maintained houses.

The track Jacob had been following widened into a street littered with garbage and other refuse. The smell of rotting vegetables mingled with the smoke from the foundries brought Jacob out of his thoughts and back into the present, making him pay attention to his surroundings again.

With the buildings came more people, dressed in ragged clothes with equally ragged patches that tugged at the threadbare material. Most of them, adults and children alike, were barefoot, and in his clean robe and leather sandals, Jacob stood out; the object of many stares and covetous looks.

Jacob had been in similar places in Jerusalem and Babylon, and knew not to meet their eyes, or appear to be hurrying. He still had the long knife strapped to his right arm, but it would be of little help against so many people if they decided they wanted his clothes or sandals.

After another fifty paces, the street joined a wider cleaner avenue that wove through palms and houses in a westerly direction toward the Euphrates and the center of Kweiresh.

The smell of smoke and burning from the foundries grew stronger the closer Jacob came to the river. At another intersection, there was an inn, and the innkeeper, a man as tall as Jacob and with a belly hanging over his waist, was standing outside the stables offering jugs of beer to anyone passing by. Jacob was almost past the man when he stopped and passed over some bronze coins.

After Jacob had sipped the tart Babylonian beer, he said to the innkeeper. "I'm looking for a foundry to build a door for my house. An acquaintance suggested Kweiresh, but didn't tell me who would do the best job. Would you have any suggestions?"

The innkeeper frowned as he filled a mug for another customer and pocketed more coins. "I'd usually tell you to go to my wife's family, but a door's too big a job for them." He scratched at his beard, and his look at Jacob was one of inspection. "One of the foundries is operated by some of your people. It's the first one on the left side as you come to the river. Why don't you try them first? They might give you a better deal," and he grinned, revealing his stained teeth.

"I'll do that," Jacob thanked him, handed back the empty mug, and continued along the avenue.

Three hundred paces further on, Jacob found himself at another intersection, and here several streets came together into an open space with more street vendors, and more people. Something about the crowd, their clothing, the buzz of their conversation was strangely familiar. And then he realized.

They were all his people.

It was the first time since the trek across the desert from Jerusalem that Jacob had been with so many other Judeans, and for a moment, it was more overwhelming than the crush of people at the Ishtar Gate. He stood to one side of the street as people wove around him, some ignoring him, others casting curious glances as he listened to the accents of Jerusalem, Bethel, and Hebron.

He turned his head as two young men brushed past him, talking rapidly in the tone of Gibeon, the town where Jacob was born. Jacob took a pace to follow the youths, but a sudden explosion of shrill and frightened cries turned him back, making him focus on the far side of the square nearest the river.

There was a flurry of movement, and the crowd surged away from the Euphrates toward Jacob. Behind the running and panicked people, he saw the flashes of sunlight reflected on helmets and drawn swords, heard the harsh, guttural tones of Akkadian.

Jacob's first instinct was to reach for a sword that wasn't there, and rush forward to protect his people. The crowd opened before him, giving him space to run forward. As he moved, Jacob saw two small children, maybe four or five years old, standing among the milling crowd, eyes wide and searching. The boy reached for his sister's hand as they were bounced and jostled and fell to the dust.

Jacob moved faster. "This way," he called, catching the attention of the two children. He waved his arm, and they scrambled to their feet, stumbling toward him. Jacob kept his focus on the children while another part of his mind saw the soldiers: Temple Guards, come into the square, and concentrate on the Judean, men who had formed a barrier to give their families the chance to escape into the side streets.

The youngest of the pair, the girl had tangled ebony hair and tears streaking dusty lines down her face as she reached Jacob. She hesitated as he reached out to help, her dark eyes suspicious and fearful.

"It's all right, Rachel," a woman's voice said behind him. "Let him show you the way."

The child came forward again, and Jacob looked up to see a young woman hurrying toward them. Jacob guessed she was maybe twenty, with hair as dark as her daughter's straggling to her shoulders. Her brown robe, patched and worn, and the lines and strain on her face made her look ten years older.

"Why are they chasing us, Mama?" the boy asked in a scared whisper.

"Because they can," she replied with a weary voice, then looked at Jacob. "Thank you. There are streets and alleys here where the Temple Guard will never find us. Don't get yourself into trouble because of us."

"Do the Temple Guards do this often?" Jacob asked.

"Often enough," she said. "Although they've left us alone for the past three or four moons. I'd ask why now, but they've never needed a reason before." She shrugged. "They're probably looking for some extra excitement during their New Year Festival."

"Maybe," Jacob agreed, and listened to the family scurry away down the alley behind him, the mother's reassuring whispers soon drowned by the noise in the square before him.

Jacob was about to go forward and join the men in their harrying tactics when a movement to his right shifted his attention. One of the Temple Guards had an arm across the chest of a Judean and had the man backed up against a wall. He was about to go to the man's aid, when the Guard glanced over his shoulder, then stepped back.

The Judean followed, his hand coming up and slapping the Guard's arm away, and revealing a profile Jacob recognized as the big laborer from Buvalu's brickworks.

The dynamic between the two men changed.

Now it was the laborer who dominated. He leaned forward as he spoke, using his fist to emphasize words Jacob couldn't hear, although the meaning was clear. The Temple Guard was being given orders. Orders he didn't like.

The brick worker finished his orders with a clenched fist that thudded into the guard's heavy leather breast plate.

The guard turned away, and Jacob quickly stepped back into the shelter of a side street before either of the two men saw and recognized him.

Instead of staying to help his fellow Judeans, Jacob knew he needed to be far from Kweiresh as quickly as possible. He'd come to Kweiresh, not sure what he'd learn.

He hadn't expected to find Zabium taking orders from a brick-yard laborer.

CHAPTER TWENTY-FOUR

The Babylonian New Year Festival
Day Nine - Afternoon

The sun was still three or four hand spans above the towers of the Esagila, as Miriam and Solly made their way through the people heading out of the city along Marduk Street. The people were mainly families, and from the fragments of conversation she overheard, they were going to rest tomorrow and return in two days for the final celebration of the New Year Festival.

Miriam estimated she had enough time to reach Samuel's home, learn what she wanted to know about the blue cord, and return before the Marduk Gate was closed for the night. It also gave her a perfect excuse to be out of the house and away from the continual barbs of her cousin's tongue.

"We need to hurry, Solly," she urged as they approached the tunnel under the city walls. "We don't want to spend the night in the Outer City."

She smiled to herself as they increased their pace, Solly almost jogging in his desire to keep up with her. Staying in the Outer City wasn't that much of a hardship and had little to do with her haste. She wanted to see Jacob again this evening and be sure he'd returned safely from Kweiresh.

Miriam was still worried about Jacob visiting Kweiresh. After Shema that morning, she had recited one of King David's psalms as an offering to keep him safe. It had the added benefit of keeping her from Esther's prying eyes and sharp tongue. She was sure Esther had breathed a sigh of relief when Miriam had asked Solly to accompany her out of the city to Samuel's home.

As Miriam had reflected on the words of the psalm, she recalled how Jacob was certain his actions were being driven by someone else, and that had made her think about the blue cord.

What if the cord found in the Esagila after the theft wasn't from a prayer shawl? What if it had some other purpose? She had some ideas herself, but decided to ask Samuel his opinion. It also gave her another chance to hold baby Enoch, and that brought another smile to her face. She and Jacob had little opportunity to talk about what happened after they married, especially where it concerned children. The idea of being pregnant scared her a little, but the thought of a little boy like Enoch excited her as well.

Which inevitably circled her thoughts back to Noah. The anger rose inside her, unbidden and dark, forcing her to clench her fists tight to stem the wail of rage she was ready to unleash. As yet, Miriam had said nothing to Isaac or Esther, but once the New Year Festival was over, there would be a reckoning. She only hoped she could keep her tone and words civil.

Miriam shook the thoughts aside and lengthened her stride again as the crowd of revelers closed around them as they entered the dark of the tunnel. The sour, bitter odor of human and animal waste clawed at her nostrils, invaded the back of her throat.

Everyone began moving a little faster in their eagerness to escape the dark and the stench, and Miriam felt herself swept up, the crush of people separating her from Solly.

She heard him call. A muffled shout that echoed above the murmur of conversation and made the smaller children cry out in fright.

Miriam turned, her eyes trying to find him in the twilight, looking for his wizened features and wispy gray beard.

As people flowed around her, hands gripped her upper arms, pinning them to her side, and a rough voice hissed in her ear.

"Don't shout or make any attempt to find help. If you do, this knife goes in all the way."

She felt the point prick through her robe and into the skin of her back, just below her ribs.

"What do you want?" she gasped, her eyes still trying to find Solly as they came closer to the tunnel exit, the half-light giving way to bright light and the road over the bridge.

There!

Except Solly slumped in the grip of two more men, their faces hidden by cloth wrapped loosely about their heads so only their eyes showed.

"What have you done to him? He's not a young man."

"The same I'll do to you unless you do as you're told," the voice hissed again. "Keep walking and not a word or a signal to the guards or the old man gets the knife. Understand?"

"Yes." It was a struggle to keep her voice even, her heart pounding, the fear churning her stomach and bringing the bile into her throat. Was this how Jacob felt when he went into battle?

There were two of them, guiding and pushing her along, across the bridge with the dark sluggish canal water in shadow below them. Once they were off the bridge, they pushed her to the left, away from Marduk Street and into one of the many side streets. It was quieter there, and after a couple of turns the one on her left jerked her to a stop.

She twisted around, deliberately trying to ignore the knife still pressed against her side. The other two were leaning Solly against the mud-brick wall of a house. He slumped back, and she saw his face twist in pain as the rough edges of the mud bricks grazed his neck and head.

"Are you awake enough to hear me, old man?" The one on her left again. He was speaking in Aramaic, and his accent was Judean. Not Jerusalem, further south if she guessed right, maybe from around Hebron or Carmel. Miriam wanted to challenge him, but knew it would be pointless. All she would do was anger him and get Solly or herself hurt. She needed to keep that information and get it to Jacob.

Miriam realized Solly was talking, his voice hoarse and weak.

"I'm awake, although my ears refuse to believe what they're hearing. What do you want of us? If you're bandits, we have nothing of value."

"I'd argue that, given what I have in my hands," the man gripping Miriam's arms said. "She's not the youngest, but there are people in Asshur who'd pay good silver for her. We're letting you go, old man, so you can carry our message."

"What message?" Solly asked, and from the quaver in his voice, Miriam could tell he hurt more than he appeared to be.

"Tell your Jacob to keep his Benjamite nose out of other people's business. We'll know if he ignores you, and if he does, what's left of her goes to Asshur."

Miriam felt the knife move away from her back, and reposition on the sleeve of her robe. As the knife ripped through the fabric, there was a noise behind them, and the man stopped, the blade sawing at the cloth.

"People." One of the other men growled in frustration. "Too many people. We'll take both of them with us."

Miriam tried to struggle and protest as the man holding her tightened his grip on her arms. She heard a swoosh of noise, followed by an explosion of pain, and everything went black.

CHAPTER TWENTY-FIVE

The Babylonian New Year Festival
Day Nine - Evening

Miriam woke reluctantly and kept her eyes closed, not quite ready to face full awareness. She wanted to believe she was in her room at Isaac's house, but it was too quiet and instead of a bed there was packed earth under her body; hard, uneven, and digging into her hips and back.

Her arms and legs were twisted and cramped, and she had a headache that was worse than any she suffered during her monthly cycle. She shifted her body and released her right hand, which had twisted under her and lost all feeling. She lifted her other hand to massage her temples and attempt to ease the throbbing pain behind her eyes. The numbness in her arm made her clumsy, and the massage was ineffective as her hand rubbed against crusted blood on her head, and she almost poked a finger into her left eye.

"Move your hand away," a woman's voice said. Miriam hesitated, then felt a firm hand grip her wrist and pull her arm away. The woman placed a strip of damp fabric on her forehead. Miriam gave a sigh of relief as the pain in her head eased a little.

Despite the dribbles of tepid water that rolled down her cheeks, Miriam opened her eyes.

The woman knelt beside Miriam, the sharp angular lines of her face creased in concern. She held another piece of damp cloth in her hand and used it to wipe the blood away from the side of Miriam's head.

"It's not bad," the woman said, in the Akkadian dialect the richer Babylonians used. She sat back on her heels and pushed a rope of long red hair back over her right shoulder. "Stay there for a while longer. I'll get you some water."

She stood and moved away with an effortless grace that allowed Miriam to see the rest of the room. The only light came from a sesame oil lamp hanging from a hook in the ceiling. From the dancing, sputtering flame of the lamp, Miriam guessed the oil was low.

The room was maybe six paces on each side with a covered window opening above her head. The door opposite where Miriam lay was cured hide secured from the outside. A block of stone to her right provided a place for a pitcher and a bundle of rags. There were no couches or places to sit, just the hard earth floor. As Miriam shifted to sit up, a fine cloud of dust rose with her, making her sneeze. She grabbed at the damp cloth as it fell away from her forehead, catching it before it hit the ground.

Another sneeze and her headache returned in full force, the pain pounding behind her eyes. Miriam squeezed her eyes closed, stifled a groan, and twisted to lean back against the mud-brick wall. The rough surface of the mud-bricks scraped her back. The distraction, although painful, was welcome. It took her thoughts away from the pain in her head and let her focus on the other person in the room.

The other woman's hair was perhaps her most striking feature.

Even in the half-light, Miriam could see the rich red color that framed the woman's face, and highlighted her high cheekbones.

"You're Inanna. Zabium's wife."

"How do you know this?" the woman asked in a husky voice tinged with a hint of fear. She backed away, and her fingers scratched along the earth floor behind her. When her hand came back into view, she gripped a sharp shard of pottery and pointed it at Miriam.

"Who are you?"

Miriam sat straighter, angling her head so what little light the lamp gave shone on her face.

"I am Miriam. You don't know me, or Jacob. Jacob is working with your husband to find you. And to find the silver and olibanum taken from the Temple of Marduk."

"You are lying. Zabium was told to tell no-one."

"And Zabium hasn't," Miriam said. "Jacob is clever. He knows when a man aches for his woman. A woman he loves, who is being held to ensure her husband does what others want him to do."

Inanna sat back on her heels, the shard of pottery loose in her fingers, and no longer aimed directly at Miriam. She studied Miriam and tilted her head to one side.

"This Jacob. He means much to you?"

"Everything."

"And do you mean as much to him?"

Miriam knew Jacob felt the same attraction for her as she did for him. She had never connected the small things before. The way his voice changed when he spoke to her. The way he seemed to know where she was whenever they were in the same place. The way his eyes changed if he thought she was at risk.

Miriam nodded. "Yes," she said. "I believe I do."

"They will use that against him, as they used it against my Zabium." She opened her mouth to add something more, but there was the noise of men from outside the building.

The hide covering was pulled aside, letting in a rush of air. The air was warm and heavy with smoke. To Miriam it felt fresh and clean, and the pain in her head subsided to a dull ache.

A man came into the room. He carried a sesame oil lamp before him in such a way that Miriam could only make out his size and shape. His face remained in the shadows, and he smelled of dust and more wood smoke.

The man tossed a knife and a small leather pouch onto the packed earth. They landed with two dull thuds as he lifted the lamp higher, and the smell of the burning sesame oil drifted around the room.

"Use the knife and cut off a piece of your hair," he said to Miriam in an accented, growling tone. "Put the hair in the pouch. Don't think about using the knife for anything else or Jacob won't like what we send back to him."

Miriam's hand trembled as she reached for the knife.

"I'll do it," Inanna said. She placed a comforting hand on Miriam's shoulder and used the other to scoop up the knife and pouch. Inanna used her long fingers to comb and smooth Miriam's hair so it was ready for the knife.

At any other time, Miriam would have welcomed someone brushing her hair. Now she gripped her hands together to stop them shaking. She struggled to keep her back straight and her head up, when she really wanted to turn away, curl up and sob. She felt a sharp tug as Inanna cut away a length of hair, then the other woman cursed, and Miriam heard the knife thud onto the earth floor again.

"Cursed thing," Inanna said. "I cut myself. It's nothing," she added as Miriam turned to help.

Drops of blood had splashed onto the strands of Miriam's hair. The dust from the floor clung to the strands, turning the black almost gray, and hiding the pieces of red hair Inanna was folding into the mass, and then into the pouch.

"Good," the man said with a laugh. "Now throw the knife back toward me, if you can do it without cutting yourself again. Now the pouch," he added as the knife landed at his feet.

The lamp moved, sending the shadows dancing as the man crouched, retrieved the knife and pouch, then backed out of the room.

The hide covering was pulled back across the doorway, and they heard the scrape of something heavy being pushed against it. The light above their heads seemed dimmer now the lamp was gone.

Miriam shuddered and let her shoulders slump forward.

CHAPTER TWENTY-SIX

The Babylonian New Year Festival
Day Nine - Evening

Jacob had come back into the city through the Sin Street gate,
stopped at his own home, and went on to Isaac's house.

"You've missed all of them," Amos said. "Isaac is at a celebration
for New Year, and Miriam took Solly to see Samuel. She said she'd be
back." He tilted his head to one side and studied Jacob.

"You have something to say. Come with me."

Amos led Jacob up the steps from the courtyard to the balcony,
and then to a ladder leaning against the wall. The rungs creaked and
groaned as Amos climbed up. Jacob followed, and on the top rung he
paused in surprise.

"What is this?"

"I reinforced the roof and added some couches," Amos said,
sweeping his arm across the rooftop. "Isaac considers me a fool, but

when I look south or east, there's nothing but the sky, and the view gives me peace."

"I should do the same," Jacob said, climbing off the top rung of the ladder and onto the roof. He felt the beams sag a little under his weight, but not enough to be alarming. It would be too hot during the day with nothing to shade the sun, but Amos was right. Looking east away from the Esagila and the royal palaces there was an uninterrupted view of the sky. It would be a good place to say Shema every morning and evening.

"I thought this would be a good place to talk," Amos said. "Sometimes these courtyards feel like a prison." He leaned back on the couch. "I think the desert will be a good place for me if our caravan to Judah ever leaves." He shifted on the couch, then leaned forward. "What did you learn in Kweiresh?"

"More than I expected," Jacob said, and told Amos about the confrontation he'd seen between Zabium and the Judean.

"You think he's working with them against Arioch?"

"I think Zabium is trapped in something beyond him. He must know Arioch would suspect, and while Zabium tolerated me at first, he's become almost obstructive in the past two days. His arrival at Aatami's workshop must have been more than coincidence, but he didn't explain why he was there."

"What are you going to do?" Amos asked.

"I..."

Jacob lost the rest of his thought when they heard a noise in the courtyard below, and the weak cry of Solly's voice.

When they reached the courtyard, Solly was slumped against the wall. He looked up as Jacob approached, tried to step forward, and stumbled. He would have fallen, but Amos was there, hooking his hands under the older man's arms, steadying him, and guiding him across the courtyard to a seat where the older man slumped down. There were scrapes and congealed blood on Solly's cheeks.

He looked frail and old.

"Sit there and rest," Amos said. "I'll get you some wine."

Solly shook his head. "Is Jacob here? I need to see Jacob."

His hand scrabbled inside his robe and he pulled out a small leather pouch the size of his palm.

"I'm here," Jacob said. He moved so Solly could see him without having to move his head.

Fear twisted Jacob's insides at the thought of what might be inside the pouch.

Solly extended his arm, offering the pouch to Jacob. "This is for you. They insisted I give it to you."

Jacob took the pouch, and felt the weight of a clay tablet inside, felt the relief wash over him. "Do you know who they are?"

Solly sipped from the wine cup Amos gave him, then took a long swallow.

"No," he said finally. "They came up behind us in the tunnel of the Marduk Gate. I didn't see any of them."

His head dropped, and his hand shook, spilling wine onto the dirt of the courtyard. "I'm sorry, Jacob. My job was to protect her, and I failed."

Jacob came forward, squatted before Solly, and placed his arm on the older man's shoulder. "They would have killed you," Jacob said. "You did the right thing." He gave a reassuring squeeze, pushed back, stood and lifted the flap of the pouch.

The tablet slid out into Jacob's hand. He felt the clay soft in his hand; the edges crumbling. It hadn't hardened completely, and he turned the tablet carefully, so he didn't disturb or damage the words etched into the clay. The letters were rough and had none of the precision Jacob had seen in contract tablets and other agreements. The edges were blurred and the Aramaic poor, but he could still read and understand the words: *Stay away and let this finish, or she dies.*

Jacob passed the tablet across to Amos, who had come up beside him, and tipped the pouch upside down. A hank of hair, matted with blood and caked with dust, dropped out into Jacob's hand. Solly winced.

"Did they hurt her?" Amos asked.

"Not that I saw," Solly said, then lifted his head as a memory came back to him. "They came on us at the Marduk Gate, and would have sent me back then, but there were too many people around. They spoke Aramaic, Jacob, and they called you a Benjaminite."

Jacob nodded his head slowly. It made sense and matched everything else he now understood. He felt a surge of hope rush through his body. He moved into the brighter circle of light from the nearest sesame oil lamp and lifted the hand holding the hair closer to his face. He inhaled slowly, and this time he couldn't keep the smile from his face.

"I don't believe Miriam's hurt," he said. "But I'm certain I know where she is, and who is with her."

"How?" There was disbelief in Amos's question.

Jacob fanned the strands of hair out across his palm. "If you look in the light, you can see there are two colors of hair. The black is Miriam's. There are also strands from a red-haired person, probably another woman. And smell it," he said, offering his hands out to Isaac.

Isaac dipped his head. "Smoke," he said after a moment. "It's very faint, but I smell smoke."

"I smelled it as well," Solly said, lifting his head, his dark eyes coming alive. "I couldn't see anything, because they put a sack over my head, but there was definitely smoke. I couldn't hear much because of the sack, but the men cursed about it." He looked across at Jacob, and his wrinkled face twisted into a brief smile. "And no, Jacob, I didn't recognize his voice."

"That would be too much to expect," Jacob said, with a smile of his own, as he curled his fingers around the hair like it gave him a connection to Miriam.

"What will you do?" Isaac said.

"Get her back."

He turned away from them and strode toward the street door.

There were few revelers in the street celebrating the end of this ninth day of the New Year Festival. Judeans occupied most of the houses here. Jacob felt his gut clench and twist at the thought of celebrating the Feast of Trumpets, the Judean New Year, without Miriam. It would be no feast.

"Jacob."

Jacob paused at the call and turned to see Amos had followed him into the street.

"What is it?"

"Do you recall when we were talking about strategy, and you realized how the people behind this theft were manipulating you about the Twar, the small people?"

"What of it?" Jacob struggled to keep his voice level. He didn't want this distraction. He wanted to rescue Miriam.

"This taking of Miriam isn't a coincidence? They know how you care for her, and that she's very special to you."

Jacob watched Amos move back a step, realizing the big man was afraid of the reaction his next words would provoke.

"Just say it," Jacob said, relaxing a fist he hadn't realized he'd clenched. "I give my word I won't hurt you."

Amos relaxed a little, but Jacob could see the wariness that remained in the man's brown eyes. "They want you unbalanced and unable to think clearly. Taking Miriam is the only way they have to unsettle you. They're afraid of you, Jacob. What was it you said to me? Use that fear and turn it against them."

Jacob frowned, then felt the laughter bubble in his throat. The sound was harsh to his ears, and without humor, but Jacob knew the words had served the purpose Amos had intended.

"Thank you," Jacob said, placing his hand on Amos's shoulder and giving a reassuring squeeze as the pieces clicked into place in his mind. "You're right, and I believe they've done the same to Zabium."

Amos nodded in agreement. "That would explain why he seems helpful at one moment and obstructive the next. If he does one thing these people don't like, they'll kill his wife. Can you save her as well?"

Jacob sighed, wondering again why it fell to him. "They're

together. On the one occasion Zabium spoke of his wife, he told me how her hair shines like copper in the sun. When we rescue Miriam, we'll find Zabium's wife as well."

CHAPTER TWENTY-SEVEN

The Babylonian New Year Festival
Day Ten - Morning and Afternoon

Jacob recited Shema alone the next morning. He hoped the focus would keep Miriam from his thoughts, and maybe if he set the pace and tone of the ritual, it would restore some of the vitality and energy he missed.

At the end, as the rising sun warmed his shoulders, Jacob had to admit the words remained dry and with no deeper meaning for him. His stomach remained twisted into a knot of fear for Miriam, and he knew when he sent Passhur to the Esagila with a message for Zabium, he would need to keep a tight rein on his temper.

The Babylonian arrived late in the morning. Jacob took him into the cool shaded room he used as a place to relax. They settled into couches covered in soft fabrics, and with the window coverings open, the room was bright and felt airy.

Zabium slumped onto the couch facing the window. He screwed

his face against the brighter light. His beard looked ragged. The angular spade shape favored by the Babylonians was barely recognizable. His dark eyes were bloodshot, and there were marks and stains on his tunic.

The man looked terrible, and Jacob guessed Zabium had slept very little in the past few days. He decided there was no point in being sensitive.

"When did they take Inanna?"

"What do you mean? Inanna's at our home."

"No, she isn't, Zabium. They took her to make sure you didn't interfere with their plans, just as they took Miriam last night. When was Inanna taken?"

Zabium protested, then thought better of it. He frowned, his shoulders slumped, and his head went down. He ran a hand through his unkempt hair. "Two or three days ago," he admitted in a dull tone. "It was the day after we visited Buvalu at the brickworks."

"Is that why you were in Kweiresh?"

"Not directly. They wanted me to talk with Aatami and make sure he didn't tell you anything. The raid was an excuse for me to get close and tell them Aatami was dead."

"Did you kill him?"

Zabium shook his head. "No, but it was probably because of me they killed him." He reached for the wine and took a long swallow. "What are you going to do?"

"Get Miriam and Inanna back," Jacob said. "Do you really believe whatever happens with the silver and olibanum, they'll live?"

"No, I don't. In my heart, I feel I've already lost her." Zabium lifted his head, and his bloodshot eyes focused on Jacob. "What are you thinking?"

"How many of your men do you trust, Zabium?"

"All of them."

Jacob shook his head. "Not for this. I'm asking you which of your men you trust enough that they'll join you even when the task could put them in conflict with the Temple."

"How? We're doing the work of the Temple by finding the silver and olibanum."

"Even if someone in the Temple is behind the theft?"

Zabium shook his head slowly again. "Being a soldier was so much easier. You think Arioch arranged this?"

"No. I don't think it was Arioch. My guess is someone inside or close to the Esagila set this up to bring Arioch down. Think about that, then tell me how many of your men you really trust."

"Not enough," the Babylonian admitted after a long silence between them. "Maybe two or three. No more than four." He shook his head, then lifted his head and looked across at Jacob. "Why can't I take in a squad of my guard?"

"Because it will cause a disturbance and get the women killed," Jacob sat back. "Until we know the silver is there, we can't officially involve the Temple. It will be bad enough if we're wrong, but using Temple resources for a personal vendetta will put Arioch in a worse position than he is now."

"You expect to be part of this, don't you?"

Jacob nodded. "Of course. Stay with your lower number, four of us will be enough." He leaned over the table and moved the platter of fruit and nuts to one side, helping himself to a handful of almonds as he did so. He put a nut in his mouth and laid the others out in the shape of a rough square.

"This is Buvalu's brickyard," he said, placing two small piles of almonds inside the square. He pointed at one pile. "That's the kiln, the other almonds are the building we were in. What else do you remember?"

They worked for nearly an hour, adding to the makeshift model with more nuts and dates to represent the lines of drying mud-bricks.

"We're missing something," Zabium said finally. "There's nothing there that would hold Inanna and Miriam. This building we were in," he pointed at the second pile of almonds Jacob had placed. "It's too small to hold them, and I saw no other buildings." Zabium paused, then pointed at the row of dates. "What was behind this stack of bricks?"

"I don't know. I'm not sure we had the chance to see anything there."

Jacob closed his eyes to better focus his thoughts on the stack of bricks.

"It was high," he said finally. "About the same height we would reach if you stood on my shoulders. There's enough room between the bricks and the far boundary wall to put a small building."

"We need better information," Buvalu said. "But neither of us can get it. They know our faces and will kill Inanna and Miriam if they see either of is."

"I know," Jacob said, and leaned back on the couch, feeling the hard wood grind into his shoulders. He let the slight pain stay, it helped focus his mind away from Miriam and what might be happening to her.

"What about Bel Ibni?"

Jacob shook his head and sat forward, picking a date from the pile representing the bricks. "He'd give himself away immediately, but Horam wouldn't. He's just inherited his grandfather's home, and replacing some bricks is a good reason to be there, even during the New Year Festival."

Hope sparked in Zabium's dark eyes. "Will he do it?"

"Let's find out," Jacob said.

The sun was well past the midday hour and into the afternoon when Horam returned. Jacob could see the result of the expedition from the grim look on the younger man's face.

"I'm sorry," Horam said. He sat on the couch opposite Jacob and Zabium, his hands moving nervously from his knees to his lap, and then folded back across his body.

"There are people at the brickworks, but no-one would talk to me. There was a tall, heavy man at the gate. He had scars on his arms and a beard like yours, Jacob. It was like he was a guard. He told me to come back after the Festival. I wanted to press him, but there was something about him that made me nervous."

"I remember him," Jacob said, recalling the confrontation he'd had with the two Judeans four days before, and the same man he'd seen talking to Zabium in Kweiresh. "You did the right thing, Horam. He has a short temper, especially toward Babylonians. Did you notice anything else?"

Horam shook his head. "Not really. The brick kiln was still operating. I could feel the heat from the gate. I suppose they have to keep it hot all the time. And a man came from behind the towers of bricks you told me about. He was carrying an empty waterskin, and he didn't look happy."

"I wouldn't be happy about running out of water in that place," Jacob agreed.

"Did the man say anything?" Zabium asked.

Horam shook his head again. "Not that I heard, although he was looking behind him. But it didn't make sense. The man at the gate told me there were only three people there. I saw him and two by the kiln. So who was the extra man, and what was he looking back at?"

Jacob felt his spirits lift. He glanced across at Zabium and saw the other man had reached the same conclusion. Jacob extended his hand and squeezed Horam's shoulder in gratitude. "He's the guard. He's the man watching Miriam and Zabium's wife."

"What are you going to do?" Horam asked.

"Get them," Jacob said, repeating the words he'd used with Zabium earlier in the day. He rose to his feet and look across at Zabium. "Tonight. Can you get your men?"

"I'll do what I can," Zabium said, also rising to his feet. "Tonight may be difficult. The priests return from the Temple of the New Year Festival tomorrow, and there's a lot of preparation."

"Do what you can," Jacob said. "If it's just you and me, then so be it. Meet me outside the Marduk Gate before the sun goes down. We don't want to be inside the city when the gates are closed."

"Do you need me to bring you a sword?"

"I have my own," Jacob said, mentally adding a pair of daggers to the sword he'd carry openly. "You bring food. We must eat because it promises to be a long night."

"And a dark one," Zabium said as he reached the door.

There was a cold impersonal note to Zabium's voice, and Jacob felt a shiver of concern twist his gut. He'd heard that tone during the siege.

It came from men who didn't want, or expect, to come back alive.

CHAPTER TWENTY-EIGHT

The Babylonian New Year Festival
Day Ten - Night

The night air was cool, with a soft breeze coming out of the north. Jacob shivered and felt the chill bumps ripple up his bare arms. He'd considered bringing a cloak, but if he really needed to use his sword, the cloak would hinder his movements.

Above him the thin sliver of the pale new moon light was almost lost in the brightness of the other stars in the dark sky. The combined light was just enough to see the length of the street from where he stood in the shadows of a house. What he could see, Jacob didn't like.

The gate to the brickworks was closed and appeared barred, as he'd expected. What he hadn't expected was the glitter and shine of ceramic shards on the top of the wall. Anyone trying to climb over the wall risked being sliced and slashed by the sharp edges. Jacob had used the same techniques in the fords and rivers of Judah to slow the Babylonian advance.

The tactics hadn't worked well enough to save Jerusalem, but they looked solid here. Zabium had only brought one man with him, the tall, lean guardsman Jacob had met at the Esagila two days before, and whose name Jacob couldn't recall. Neither of the Babylonians wore their leather armor, which surprised Jacob, until he remembered how it weighed on the shoulders, slowed you down and restricted rapid movement.

It made sense to him now. They needed the element of surprise more than ever now they knew they'd be outnumbered by at least one, probably two men.

Jacob didn't think there was a watchman, but because he had seen no one didn't mean there wasn't someone watching the street. Slowly, Jacob eased himself back round the corner of the house to where Zabium and the other soldier waited.

Quickly Jacob relayed what he'd seen, and what it meant for their plan for him to climb the wall and open the gate from the inside.

Zabium let out a low growl of frustration. The other man, Ligish. Jacob remembered his name now. Ligish smiled with a flash of white teeth and reached to his throat for the clasp of his cloak.

"It's an inconvenience, but nothing we cannot overcome. Fold the cloak, place it over the pottery on the wall and it will protect you."

Jacob took the cloak, feeling the weight and quality of the fabric. "Are you certain? It could ruin your cloak."

"It's just a cloak," Ligish said with another smile. "I lost count of how many I destroyed protecting the hooves of the animals whenever we forded a stream or river during the Judah campaign. I can always get a replacement, unless the night goes against us, and then it won't matter."

Jacob smiled at the veteran's calm acceptance of what might be before them. He'd said his own prayers before he left the city and sent a tablet of instructions to Amos. Just in case.

Jacob placed the folded cloak across his right shoulder, checked the gate and sprinted across the road to the corner of the wall surrounding the brickworks. Behind him he heard the scuff of sandals

dislodging stone on the earth surface of the street, then the two Babylonians were beside him.

The three of them moved like they'd worked together for many
years. Zabium and Ligish crouched and made cups with their hands,
allowing Jacob to step in and reach for the top of the wall.

The mud and clay on the top of the wall crumbled as Jacob
hooked his hands over the edge. The dust drifted into his nose and
throat and he felt the overwhelming desire to sneeze. He forced
himself to stop breathing, and attempted to ignore the tickle in his
nostrils as he lifted the cloak from his shoulder, and draped it over the
wicked-looking spikes of the pottery shards.

Quickly, Jacob levered himself up onto the top of the wall, and
was sure he heard sighs of relief from Zabium and Ligish hidden in
the dark shadows below him. He crouched low on the wall, and
looked out over the interior of the brickworks, searching for any signs
of life or movement.

When he saw and heard nothing, Jacob moved carefully to the far
edge of the wall, and swung himself down. The dry mud-brick fell
apart as his weight came on his hands. His left hand slipped. The
sword scabbard thudded against the wall. His weakened right hand
couldn't take the sudden weight and Jacob tumbled down, landing on
his back.

The air whooshed out of his lungs, and he lay there for a moment,
one part of him trying to suck the smoke laden air into his body, the
other attempting to roll over and reach the sword in case anyone
came to investigate the noise.

It seemed forever, but Jacob knew only a few minutes had passed
by the time he could breathe properly again. He stood slowly,
brushed the dust off his arms and hands, and drew the sword.

The small building where he and Zabium had met with Buvalu
was just in front of him, a dark silent bulk in the starlight. The gate
was maybe thirty paces beyond the building on the left side. The
towers of bricks off to his right had a ruddy, scarlet hue to them that
came from the kiln.

Jacob reached the corner of the building and glanced quickly across the open space toward the kiln. Two men were working the fire and the pile of bricks waiting to be fired. They had their backs to him as they stoked the fire, stepping to one side when the flames billowed out, casting orange light over everything. One man cursed. Jacob caught the Aramaic words and knew who the man was.

Two men by the fire. No one in the hut behind him. That left the others on the far side of the brick stack. Jacob felt the slick twist of his stomach at the thought of what those men might do to Miriam and Inanna. He pushed the thought away. It was a distraction that could get him killed.

Stacked against the wall beside the gate were more bricks, their edges ragged and crumbling. The edges crumbled even further as Jacob touched them. Dust flaked away and something silvery flashed brightly in the light from the kiln.

Something nagged at the edge of Jacob's mind, but he put the concern aside as he reached the gate. It surprised him to find the two sides closed with nothing securing them. He and the Babylonians could have pushed them open and walked in.

The gate scraped on the earth as Jacob pulled it open. Not a loud noise, but enough to make him glance over at the kiln where the two Judeans made no sign they'd heard the noise.

Zabium and Ligish slipped in through the gate. Jacob pointed to the kiln, and Ligish moved to his right to cover them. As they'd planned, Jacob and Zabium headed for the left end of the brick pile.

They were nearly halfway there when a man came from the far side of the bricks. Jacob recognized Buvalu.

Buvalu saw them at the same time. He started forward, drawing his sword and lowering his head as he bellowed a warning to the men working the kiln.

"Help Ligish," Jacob ordered, and stepped into the path of Buvalu's headlong charge.

Their swords clashed and Jacob turned away, wishing he had a shield to protect his right side. Buvalu backed away a pace. His face twisted in a combination of anger and concentration, and Jacob guessed the man had rarely fought a left-hander before. It unsettled those not trained for it.

As Jacob parried a wild slash, he heard the clash of metal as Zabium and Ligish engaged their opponents. He worried about the fourth man, and if there was a fifth somewhere in the dark shadows.

Buvalu's fighting technique depended more on his strength and brute force rather than any actual skill. He wielded his sword more like a club than an edged weapon. It was easy for Jacob to avoid the wild swings, but there was no immediate way he could close and finish the fight without exposing himself to Buvalu's huge arms and hands.

A pace back as the sword whirled across Jacob's front. His foot caught on a stone, turning his ankle. Jacob stumbled, going down onto one knee, barely having time to raise his arm and hold the sword horizontal to parry the clubbing blow Buvalu aimed.

Jacob let himself fall back, rolling away, his right hand in the dirt and ash as he spun to his feet, skipping to the left as Buvalu swung again, then tossing the dust out of his right hand. Buvalu jerked his head back, his left hand coming up to avoid the cloud. Jacob swung round and down, his blade thudding into Buvalu's wrist with the same meaty thud a butcher's blade made when breaking up a carcass.

Buvalu wasn't feeling the pain yet, but the surprise and shock made him hesitate. Jacob surged forward, closing with the Babylonia, his knee lifting hard into the man's groin, and as Buvalu fell back, Jacob executed the reverse slash across the man's throat.

He stood for a moment, breathing heavily

A woman screamed. The shrill noise cut through the grunting and snarling of the men fighting. Out of the corner of his eye, Jacob saw Zabium hesitate. He'd recognized the owner of the voice, and the angle of his parrying stroke wavered. It was the opening Zabium's opponent needed.

Time slowed.

Jacob raised his sword, starting to run.

He watched helplessly as the renegade Judean's sword slashed down and across, ripping through Zabium's tunic in a diagonal slice that opened him from right shoulder to just above the waist on his left side.

Zabium let out a surprised cry that sounded like a hacking cough. He dropped his sword, and his head slumped down.

Jacob's sword drove into the Judean's stomach as he started his killing blow. The force drove the man back. Jacob also stepped back, freeing his sword from the man's belly, then slashing it across his throat.

Jacob glanced across at Ligish, who had just dispatched the third man. Their eyes locked. They reached Zabium at the same time. Ligish dropped to his knees. In the reddish light from the flames of the kiln, Jacob saw his dark face go pale. When he looked down at Zabium, he saw why. In the half-light, the blood pulsing from Zabium's chest looked black as it soaked onto the tunic and dribbled down his side into the dust.

"Don't move him," Jacob commanded. He dropped his sword in the dust and began running for the end of the stack of bricks.

"Miriam!" Jacob yelled as he rounded the corner and almost barreled into two figures creeping along the edge of the stack.

"Jacob?"

He grabbed her, pulling her away from the other woman and into his arms, reveling in the solid warmth and life in her as she clung to him with equal passion.

"I need your skill," he said, reluctant to let her go, but knowing he had to.

"What is it?"

He leaned in close, trying to ignore the scent of her. "Zabium's hurt," he murmured. "Badly."

He felt her head nod against his chest. "Look after Inanna," she said, breaking their embrace and running away from him.

"What happened? Where's Zabium?"

Inanna's voice quavered, and as Jacob went to her, he could see in the starlight she was trembling.

"He's hurt." Jacob said. "Miriam will do all she can for him, but they'll both need your help." He took her arm and led her slowly back to the front of the brickworks where Miriam was already on her knees beside Zabium.

She turned and looked up at Jacob. "I need light, cloth, and boiling water. And we need to move him."

"There, or where they imprisoned you?" Jacob asked, pointing to the building beside the kiln as he retrieved his sword, and used Buvalu's robe to wipe it clean.

"There," Miriam replied. "I want to move him as little as possible."

Jacob and Ligish cleared a space in the room, pushing tablets and scrolls aside and having little concern about anything they broke or ruined. Zabium lost consciousness as they moved him, and Jacob thought that was the best thing for him.

As Miriam used one of Jacob's knives to cut away the rest of Zabium's tunic, Jacob took Ligish to one side.

"I need you to go to the Temple of the New Year Festival. I don't care what it takes, but you need to get to Arioch and the Temple Guard. The silver and olibanum are here, and Arioch needs to get them back to the Esagila."

Ligish looked back into the room where Miriam had three lamps burning and was tying strips of cloth around Zabium's shoulder to slow the bleeding.

"Bring me dates, or figs," she called without pausing in her work. "And hurry."

CHAPTER TWENTY-NINE

The Babylonian New Year Festival
Day Ten - Night

Jacob left Miriam and Inanna tending to Zabium. Around him the brick yard was dark with just the noise of the fire in the kiln crackling and spitting red and yellow sparks into the air. Jacob checked the bodies and searched the compound once more to be certain no one else was hiding. Finally, he returned to the pile of bricks he'd looked at before letting Zabium and Ligish into the compound.

In the dim light from the moon, Jacob studied the pile for a while before he picked a brick from the stack. The poorly cured clay crumbled into a gritty dust beneath his fingers, but the brick still felt heavier than usual. Jacob brushed away more of the dried mud dust, his fingers coming up against something hard and unyielding. He brushed more dirt away and was rewarded with the shine of silver in the moonlight.

Jacob remembered the knowing smirk Buvalu had aimed at him

when their paths had crossed in the Temple hallways two days before. He shook his head.

"He moved the silver in plain sight, and right past all of us," Jacob said in a soft whisper.

"You sound impressed," Miriam said, coming up beside him.

Jacob placed the block of silver back onto the pile of bricks and drew Miriam into his arms.

"Are you all right?"

He felt her nod into his chest. "I was scared, but I knew you'd find us. You still sounded impressed."

"I am," Jacob admitted. "Buvalu walked right past Arioch, Zabium, and me with the silver hidden inside these bricks. He had to have help from inside the Esagila?"

"Zabium?"

Jacob shook his head. "Zabium suspected something, so they took Inanna to keep him under control. Like they tried to do with you."

"Arioch won't be pleased."

"I think he suspects, or already knows," Jacob said. "What will frustrate him most is not knowing who Buvalu was working for."

It was another two hours, and the moon had nearly set when Ligish returned, not just with Arioch but a full detachment of the Temple Guard who looked to Ligish for direction.

Their first task was to deliver the figs to Miriam, then secure the silver.

"Leave a guard on the silver, and we'll get it back to the Esagila at first light," Arioch ordered Ligish. His voice was tired, his pace slow as he came and stood beside Jacob.

They watched as Miriam spooned a hot poultice of the figs and water onto a long strip of cloth. She rolled the cloth into a long tube, carefully tucking in the ends so the mixture couldn't leak out. Miriam gestured to Inanna, who moved behind her husband's head and placed her hands on his upper arms.

"It might be better if she lets him die there," Arioch said. "It will save the Temple the cost of an execution."

"He saved your life, and livelihood. Cooperating with Buvalu was Zabium's only chance to save his wife," Jacob said.

"Which would not have been necessary if he hadn't betrayed me earlier." Arioch folded his arms into the sleeves of his robe. "When I consider that his inaction, if successful, would have laid the blame firmly on your people, I find your defense of him intriguing. You realize Buvalu wasn't working alone."

Jacob nodded, then realized in the dim light, Arioch couldn't see the movement. "I suspected as much, but I think our trail stops here?"

"What about the blue cord?"

"A coincidence. One of Buvalu's Judean workers used the cord to tie his hair back. It fell out in the storeroom. Like the other Judeans, he was following Buvalu's orders and had no choice. My people don't have that sort of freedom, Arioch."

The priest sighed. "You seem to do well enough, Jacob, but I take your point. I also understand Zabium's motives, although it will do him no good. Inanna's life is forfeit as well. Zabium knew that when he became my Guard Commander."

Jacob sighed, then winced as Miriam applied the hot poultice to Zabium's chest. The Babylonian let out a high scream of pain that caused some of the Guards to pause and look around.

Inanna released Zabium's shoulders as the cry fell away to a bubbling murmur. She turned away, putting her hands to her face, unable to hide the tears streaming down her cheeks.

Arioch slapped at a cinder that landed on his robe, brushing it away before it could mark the cloth. "Zabium will be a loss," he continued. "I wanted to reward him for his actions against the bandits who attacked one of the Temple's caravans. Perhaps I should have left him doing what he loved."

Around them, the Temple Guards stood protectively over the stack of bricks that held the stolen silver. Others checked the buildings a second or third time to make certain no-one still hid there. From the jovial calls, and relaxed way they now held their weapons, Jacob could see they didn't expect to find anyone.

"Maybe he should die here," Jacob said in a low voice. "With that shoulder wound, I doubt he'll be able to use a sword effectively again. It would be a gesture of your mercy to banish his family rather than execute them."

"Your woman Miriam will not like that. Will you kill him, or do you expect me to do it?"

Jacob nodded toward the bodies the guards had piled beside the kiln. "Neither of us. There's one of those bodies close enough that we could make it look like Zabium."

"And you get what from this?"

"I need. Bel Ibni, needs a caravan master. Zartok and his family came from Asshur looking for a new start after a family disagreement. He won't need to come inside the Inner Walls of the city very often, and probably never to the Temple of Marduk."

"You do not think the weight of gratitude will become a burden to him? Zabium, Zartok, is a proud man."

"He won't be a slave, or indentured, Arioch. I need someone to get a caravan to Jerusalem and back. If he wants to move on after that, I won't stop him."

Arioch inclined his head briefly in agreement. "Let us see if he survives the night. He may take the decision out of our hands. You need to manage the substitution. After this, I'm even less sure who to trust inside the Temple." He waved his hand around the brickworks. "I will leave you to arrange everything."

Jacob watched the priest stride away, issuing orders as he went. His voice was firm and authoritative. There was none of the earlier doubt as he called Ligish and another of the guards to him, and they began their journey back to the Temple of the New Year Festival for the rest of the night.

When Arioch and his entourage had left, Jacob stepped into the small room and pulled the ox-hide across the doorway, shutting them off from everyone outside.

Inanna sat on the dirt floor, clutching Zabium's hand and talking to him in a low tone Jacob couldn't hear. Beyond them, Miriam squatted on a low stool, arms on her knees, and head lowered onto her arms.

The scraping noise of the hide made Miriam lift her head. She struggled to her feet when she saw Jacob and walked into his arms. As he pulled her in close to, Jacob could see the tiredness under her eyes, the bruise high on her right cheek. He hoped Buvalu had caused the bruise. He didn't like to think someone else had killed the man who did that to her.

"How is he?" Jacob asked.

"It seems I will live," Zabium answered for Miriam, his voice stronger than Jacob expected. "At least for the moment, and long enough to return to the Temple for an execution."

"Let's talk about that," Jacob said.

Quickly he told them of his conversation with Arioch.

"Do I have a choice?" Zabium asked when Jacob had finished.

"There are always choices," Miriam said. "Execution, or the caravan are just two of them. You're not well enough to travel yet, but when you are, if you want a different option, Jacob and I will get you away from Babylon."

Zabium and Inanna exchanged a look. The small nods they gave to each other would have been easy to miss if Jacob hadn't been looking for them. "Your caravan is a good option, Jacob. Thank you."

CHAPTER THIRTY

The Babylonian New Year Festival
Day Eleven - Afternoon and Evening

Jacob and Miriam had dozed at the brickworks, then accompanied Zabium and Inanna to a room at Samuel's home, and slept longer there.

It was early afternoon before they returned to Isaac's home to find Bel Ibni and Horam in the courtyard, and the servants trying to offer platters and jugs of wine.

"You're just in time," Isaac said, eyeing their dusty robes and the sword still strapped to Jacob's waist without comment. "It seems Bel Ibni has had a delivery from the Esagila that also concerns us."

"Is it some silver?" Jacob asked with a smile.

"I doubt it," Bel Ibni said. "I saved opening the message until we were all together." He pushed his thumbnail into the seal, cracking the wax with a sharp snap, and allowing the papyrus cylinder to unroll.

Bel Ibni squinted at the marks, his mouth moving as he translated the hieroglyphs into groups of words.

He lowered the scroll and looked across at Jacob, then Isaac. "It seems we are invited to the New Year banquet at the Esagila this evening. It is also suggested. I like that, don't you, Jacob? It is also suggested, that my Judean partners and their families accompany me."

Jacob allowed himself a brief smile. "It sounds like one of those suggestions you treat as a directive."

"That is Arioch's way." Bel Ibni agreed and allowed the papyrus to roll itself back into a tube. He placed it carefully on the table and accepted the goblet of wine Amos gave him and took a long swallow. "I suspect it's Arioch's way of thanking you without provoking his enemies."

"After the last few days, I doubt they need any provocation," Jacob said, sipping slowly from his own goblet. He was still tired from the previous night and doubted the one coming would be any less stressful. "Is there a time specified for the banquet?"

Bel Ibni laughed. "Not early, I can assure you. The king and the priests and their entourages have been celebrating late into the night for the last four days. The procession from the Temple of the New Year Festival won't begin for another hour. If we arrive at the Esagila around sundown, it will be early enough. I suggest we meet at my house first, as it will be easier to get in if we arrive at the same time as a group."

After they'd said their farewells, and agreed on the meeting at Bel Ibni's home, Jacob followed Horam and his father out of Isaac's house and into the street.

"If you hear me say things this evening that disturb you," Jacob said to Bel Ibni. "Do not be concerned. There are some things that must be said. My commitment to our agreement is unchanged."

Bel Ibni gave Jacob a sharp look, then his fleshy face twisted into a huge smile. "It is long past the time you put Isaac in his place. I will enjoy watching that conversation."

The guards outside the Esagila checked Bel Ibni's scroll against another, and then a third, before allowing them inside where they were passed to a Temple acolyte who led them toward their designated table. It was a slow procession as they greeted several groups, including the family of Horam's fiance, Damkina. Seated on the far side of the group was a thin, swarthy man, whose dark eyes widened a little when he saw Jacob. Jacob saw the recognition on Tiglath's face and inclined his head slightly. The other man returned the gesture, then returned his focus to his companions.

"What was that about?" Amos asked.

"A long story, and one for another time," Jacob said as they reached the long table assigned to them on the edge of the courtyard, with no-one behind them, and with excellent views of the main tables on a raised dais where priests and members of Nebuchadnezzar's court were already sampling the first of the many courses and wine offerings.

Their party shuffled around, and Jacob made his way to the far side closest to the walls. From there he had a view of two-thirds of the area, and no-one could approach from somewhere he couldn't see.

"Here, Miriam. You sit with us." There was a shrill note in Esther's command as she pointed at a seat on the far side of where Esther was positioning her children.

Jacob watched as Miriam paused, then turned slowly and deliberately so her cousin had to meet her gaze.

"No," Miriam said as she smoothed the creases from the sleeves of her dark red robe. She spoke in a clear voice pitched so no-one could miss her words amongst the noise and chatter of the hundreds of other guests in the Esagila courtyard.

"The bride price has been placed in Ezra's care. I will sit with the man who is to be my husband," she turned her back to Esther, and continued walking until she stood close beside Jacob. He could feel the tremble of her arm through the wool of her robe. He reached down, tangling her fingers in his, and giving them a reassuring squeeze.

There was a stunned and horrified look on Esther's face, and quiet amusement on Bel Ibni's.

Jacob worked to keep his own face neutral. There was nothing he needed to say to Isaac now. Miriam had said it for both of them.

"Now we've settled that," Bel Ibni said in a cheerful voice. "Let us focus on celebrating the New Year. A year I hope will be profitable for all of us."

They were barely seated when the first food arrived.

"You're not comfortable here, are you?" Miriam said after the eighth, or was it the ninth platter of food was replaced with small plates of fruit.

Jacob turned his head and looked over at Miriam, wondering as he did frequently, how she knew him so well.

He kept his voice as low as hers. "Why do you say that?"

"You sit and stand the right way, and say all the right words, but your eyes are never still. It's like you're waiting for something bad to happen."

"We don't belong here," Jacob said. "Just being part of these ceremonies feels like idolatry. It disturbs me that our king, who should lead us and set an example, is so involved in these events. Does he not understand this is more than a celebration of their New Year? Akitu is as important to the Babylonians as the Feast of Trumpets is to us. Why else would the Babylonians make such an event of bringing the image of Nabu from Borsippa?"

"Arioch considers it an honor to have you here. It's his way of thanking you."

"The permits for Amos to travel with the caravan to Judah would have been enough," Jacob said, but she was right and he knew it.

Jacob pushed the plate of fruit away. "I don't care if the next serving is Anatolian honey," he said. "I can't eat anything more."

Beside him. Miriam did the same with her platter, and leaned back in her seat, exhaling a soft sigh. "You could feed half the city with the food here."

"What remains will be distributed to those outside the Esagila, and those who could not be part of the celebrations tonight," said a voice behind them.

Jacob turned in his seat as Miriam twisted in hers. Their legs tangled, and once again he felt the spark of connection between them. In the flare of the torches, he watched the rose flush suffuse her olive cheeks.

When Jacob focused again, a Temple acolyte was standing behind them. He was maybe fourteen years old, but already his eyes were weary with the constant cycles of rituals and learning. There was an impassive look on his tired face, and already there were lines forming around the edges of his mouth and his eyes.

"I am told the idea came from your former king, Jehoiachin," the acolyte said, then seemed to remember himself. He bowed slightly and focused his attention on Jacob.

"Priest Arioch has requested a moment of your time, Jacob of Judah."

Like the "suggestion" in the invitation to Bel Ibni, Jacob suspected this "request" had no options either.

Jacob stood and looked across the table to Isaac, then switched his speech to their native Aramaic. "If I've not returned when you leave, keep Miriam safe." He looked back at the acolyte and changed his speech to Akkadian. "Show me the way."

Jacob followed the acolyte as he threaded his way between the maze of tables until they reached the covered walkway on the edge of the courtyard.

The young man quickened his pace, his white tunic flaring at the edges as he led Jacob to the south-western corner, where he approached a doorway with two of the Temple Guard standing at attention.

The junior guard frowned at the acolyte.

"He is to meet with Arioch," the young man said and pushed forward, elbowing the guard aside.

The soldier's eye went wide and instinctively, he reached for the sword strapped to his waist.

The senior guard reached his hand across, stopping his companion from drawing the weapon. It was Ligish, the same soldier who'd accompanied Zabium the previous evening, and who now wore the insignia of Arioch's Guard Commander.

"I know this man. This is Jacob the Judean. He worked with Arioch and Zabium to solve the theft of the silver and olibanum."

Reluctantly, the younger guard released his hold on the sword and stepped back to allow Jacob and the acolyte space to enter. As Jacob stepped through the doorway, Ligish reached out and placed a restraining hand on Jacob's chest. His amused smile made Jacob relax a little.

"The young ones are always so intense," Ligish said, then leaned forward and lowered his voice so only Jacob could hear him. "I heard what you did for Zabium. He's a good man. Thank you."

The inner room was lit with lamps and the smell of the burning sesame oil was heavy in the air. Arioch was still in the fine robes he'd worn when presenting the Priestess of Sin with the gifts of silver and olibanum. His back was to Jacob and his focus was on something happening at the feast below.

The acolyte coughed politely. "I have Jacob the Judean your excellency."

"Thank you," Arioch said without turning. "Leave us."

Arioch waited until the heavy door swung closed behind the acolyte. Only then did he turn, the colors in the robe shimmering as they caught the light from the flickering lamps. "The Priestess was very pleased with the gifts," Arioch said. "Finding myself in your debt seems to be a regular event these last few moon cycles."

Jacob shook his head. "Think of it more that our mutual interests align. I'm sure there are others in Babylon who share your views."

"I'm not sure I share your optimism," Arioch said, waving Jacob to a couch with wine and fruit laid out. "Help yourself. I've celebrated so much in the past days, I could fast for a week and not be hungry." He dropped onto another couch and leaned back with a heavy sigh.

Jacob could see the fatigue in his eyes and the lines creasing his forehead.

Arioch sat forward, reached for the jug of wine and poured for them both, then took a long drink from his own goblet. "I'm guilty of a certain arrogance that surprises even me," he said, drinking again then refilling his goblet. He offered the jug to Jacob.

"Not for me."

"Probably wise," Arioch sat back, holding the wine close to his chest, like a mother protecting her child. "Where was I?"

"Something about arrogance."

The priest nodded slowly, his eyes becoming heavy, and Jacob could see the excesses of the past days were catching up with Arioch.

"I believed no one could challenge me here in the Temple. Our trading keeps us well fed and allows for extras. I should have realized others would be jealous and seek the position for themselves. The people who approached Bel Ibni really were from Harran, and from the Temple of Sin. The only untruth they told was that they had my blessing. Will you tell him?"

"I don't think so," Jacob said. "Bel Ibni has a similar arrogance problem."

Arioch laughed then, his head thrown back, the noise filling the room, and drowning the chatter from the courtyard for a moment until the priest became serious again. "The people from Harran had encouragement from someone here. Someone inside the Esagila." He held up his hand as Jacob opened his mouth to speak. "No. I suspect we have the same names on our lips, but these walls hear more than they should. We'll talk of it another time."

"And our caravan?"

Arioch gestured toward two clay tablets on the far side of the food plates. "The High Priest and the King's advisors are much happier a Babylonian is in charge of your venture. There is one permit for Amos, and a second for Eli and his family. The mark on each tablet is that of the Esagila, rather than my personal seal. Make certain Amos and Eli return to Babylon, Jacob, because it is the High Priest who will look for reparations if they don't."

"They'll return," Jacob said, reaching for the tablets. "Amos has a wedding to attend."

Arioch laughed again and lifted his goblet toward Jacob. "I'll marry the two of you tomorrow in front of whichever of our gods you choose."

Jacob felt an energy ripple through his body. In his mind he saw the shawl Miriam had repaired, the new blue cord glowing like fire. Words echoed in his head. *Tell your people to put a blue cord on the fringes of their garments so you shall remember I am the Lord your Yahweh who brought you out of Egypt.*

"Thank you for the offer. Miriam and I will consider it," Jacob said, turning back to the door as the other verses of Shema pulsed through his mind.

ABOUT THE AUTHOR

International selling author Richard Freeborn writes in many genres from historical and mystery to romance and thrillers.

Currently Richard writes stories in several series including historical mysteries set in Ancient Babylon, the Dune Crest current day mysteries, the time travel Puzzle Store series, and contemporary romances set in Diamond Beach, somewhere along Florida's panhandle.

For more information about Richard's books and projects, please visit his website at https://www.richardfreeborn.com

You can find Richard's books here: books2read.com/RichardFreeborn/

COMING SOON

The Corpse in the Courtyard

Prolog

The fifteenth day of Simanu - Afternoon

The army camp at Borsippa, a half-day ride west of the city of Babylon, was a sprawling mass of tents, storehouses, stables, and men marching, training, and hurrying from one place to another.

There was a constant cloud of dust that hung on the air, covering everything with a film of beige dust.

Ligish, Commander of the Guard at the Esagila, the temple complex that oversaw the religious life of Babylon, kept a cloth over his face. He walked his horse along the tent line, careful to avoid the web of ropes and stakes that kept the tents from collapsing.

At the end of the tent line, a pair of sentries watched followed his approach. They checked on him but also watched either side, not allowing his approach to distract them from any other potential danger.

Ligish nodded in approval. These men knew their job.

There were rumors in Babylon - in the Esagila, and even the Court of King Nebuchadnezzar - that the long campaign in Lebanon had drained the military. The army was not what it once had been, the rumors said.

Any new conflict would find them wanting.

In Ligish's opinion, the rumors were the gossip of idle tongues. The same was said of the army before the siege of Jerusalem and the subjugation of the Judeans. Ligish suspected it had been the same forty or more years before when Babylon and Elam joined forces to defeat the Assyrians and sack Nineveh.

The clash of spears being brought down across his path pulled Ligish from his thoughts.

"What is your business with the general?" The older of the two guards demanded. He looked barely twenty summers, but Ligish knew the dark empty look in his eyes.

Too many battles. Too many deaths.

Ligish hoped the guards saw something different in his own eyes, but suspected they saw the same dark empty look.

He pulled a round, gold token from a pocket his tunic, leaned down and offered it to the guard. "I am Ligish of the Esagila. I am sent by Priest Arioch to ask a favor of your general."

The guard shifted the spear upright so he could control it better, then leaned forward to study the token more closely. Whatever he saw in the symbols satisfied him. He gave a hand signal to his companion and the two soldiers stood aside.

"You must walk from here. The officer at the third tent will take you further."

Ligish replaced the token in his tunic, dismounted.

General Nebuzaraddan's tent was really two large tents joined together. One for sleeping in, the other for administrative work. A wide awning covered the front of both tents. Under the awning were two couches with straw-filled cushions, and an iron brazier, cold now in the heat of summer, but essential if a campaign ran into autumn and winter.

The layout was familiar to Ligish. He remembered it from the Judah campaign, and the first thrusts into Lebanon once the deportations from Jerusalem began.

"Ligish. I'd like to think you're here to beg me for a return to real soldiering, but your fancy uniform makes me believe otherwise."

Ligish turned at the voice behind him. Nebuzaraddan looked much the same as he had when Ligish served under him. Iron-gray hair trimmed close to his head, his spade-shaped beard trimmed shorter than the current fashion, and gray eyes that assessed under the sparkle of pleasure at seeing Ligish.

"There are times I would welcome a simple charge into the swords and spears of a known enemy." Ligish said, returning the General's hug of welcome.

"I warned you," Nebuzaraddan said as an orderly ducked his head and came under the awning with a tray of fruit and a jug of wine.

Nebuzaraddan waved toward the couches. "I have time to reminisce with an old comrade, but first tell me what Arioch wants."

"We have a situation at the Esagila," Ligish said, accepting a goblet of wine. "At the last New Year Festival, silver was stolen from inside the Esagila. We found the thieves, but not those behind the thieves. More recently two shipments of grain to the Eanna temple were spoiled, and we found vermin in the storerooms."

"Aimed at Arioch or the Esagila in general?"

Ligish shrugged. "I don't know. My belief is these are attacks with a goal to remove Arioch. I think it's someone inside the Esagila, but I can't prove it and I can't trust anyone."

Nebuzaraddan frowned over the rim of his own wine goblet.

"And I can help you how?"

"You have one of the Judean Exiles training skirmishers and groups that disrupt an enemy. He was recommended by one of his countrymen. I want to borrow Asher to find these people for me."

Nebuzaraddan frowned again, took a sip of his wine, and nodded to himself. Ligish could never interpret the look on Nezaruddan's face. He felt his stomach twist, partly anticipation and partly fear his request would be denied.

The general nodded again. "Very well, but with two conditions, Ligish. Asher must agree to this, and I want him back within four moons. The King is considering an invasion of Egypt and I will need Asher's skills for that." He reached for the wine jug and refilled their goblets. "Now tell me how what's happening with your family."

Chapter One

Two months later

The fourth day of Abu - Early Morning

Jacob woke the way he always did. A transition from sleep to awareness without the fuzzy half-asleep twilight that many people experienced. He only had that happen when wounded or injured, and didn't miss the experience.

He lay there. He felt unsettled, but couldn't work out why. After a moment, he pushed the thoughts away and rolled over to his right side. The straw mattress rustled under him, some sharp ends poking at his ribs. Jacob ignored them and pushed the thin wool blanket off his chest and stomach, trying to get some air across his body.

It was mid-summer here in Babylon, and an oppressive heat had settled over the city three days before. Night time offered no relief and on each successive day the heat felt worse.

The heat made it impossible to work outside for most of the day. Jacob had attempted it, and nearly fallen from the roof of the house he was building. He shook his head and smiled at the memory.

Not his best moment.

Thankfully he managed to hook his arm round a piece of wood and avoid a serious fall. The house stood alone between the Inner and Outer walls of Babylon, shielded from its neighbors by fruit orchards. If Jacob had fallen, it was unlikely anyone would hear his cries.

Not like Jerusalem, where inside or outside the city walls, it seemed everyone knew everyone's business.

Jacob shifted his body again as nostalgia twisted his stomach. It was five long years since the Judeans had been forced into Exile by their Babylonian conquerors. He missed Jerusalem, the city of his birth, as much now as he had in those first months. Located high above the Judean plains, Jerusalem in mid-summer was a much cooler and more pleasant place to live.

Jacob had built the house with the courtyard facing north so it received the benefit of the prevailing wind for most of the year. Of course at this time of year when the weather was hottest, the prevailing wind shifted to come from the west. He smiled at that thought and considered the progress made over the past month.

When the house was finished, this room where he lay would be for guests. The open doorway giving access to the expansive courtyard that looked over orchards and small fields of corn and barley. Three other bedrooms completed this side of the house. One was for himself and Miriam, the woman he expected to marry within the next two moons. The others for the children he hoped for, although he had barely discussed the possibility with Miriam.

They were at least ten years older than other couples beginning a marriage, so perhaps there would be no children in their future. If that was the case, the rooms would be for guests.

There was a slight fading of the night through the open doorway, and a thin rind of light creeping north from the eastern horizon.

Jacob estimated it was maybe an hour before sunrise, possibly a little longer. The time worried Jacob. He usually woke closer to the dawn, leaving himself enough time to dress and greet the rising sun with the morning Shema prayer. It was too early for the birds to be moving in the orchards, and no noise from the rooster in the house nearly a hundred paces away.

The unsettled feeling returned, and now Jacob knew why.

Something, or someone, had disturbed him.

Jacob rolled off the mattress, slipped into tunic and trews, pulled a short sword from the scabbard underneath his mattress, and hefted it in his left hand, accustoming his arm to the weight and balance.

Before the Exile, he had been a soldier. The habits he had learned a dozen years ago, as a teenager remained with him.

Jacob crouched low and eased out of the room into the courtyard. He moved slowly, a handspan at a time, in case someone watched the house. The westerly wind, barely a breeze, eddied over the roof, and moved the hot air from one place to another, providing no relief, bringing with it the heat smell like an empty pot left over a fire for too long.

He saw no movement, heard nothing except the chatter of the insects now he was out in the open. The insect hum told Jacob whoever, or whatever had been here was gone. He relaxed a small amount, but kept the sword at the ready as he let his gaze travel over the house.

To his right, the house was almost finished. There was still work needed to cover the mud-brick walls, and Jacob wanted to add proper wooden doors rather than the cured hide panels the Babylonians favored.

On the left, with walls barely above waist height were the two rooms he considered the most important. The nearest room was Miriam's workroom where she could dry herbs, and prepare the many different salves and tonics that many of the Exiles, especially the women, asked her to mix.

Next to Miriam's workroom was the kitchen. Jacob didn't want a kitchen capable of preparing huge feasts. He did want a kitchen large enough to cook for ten or twenty people so he could repay the hospitality many Exiles and Babylonians had shown him over the five years of Exile.

There were piles of mud-bricks and lengths of Lebanese cedar stacked beside the walls. Everything angular and sharp edged as it should be.

A part of Jacob wanted to relax, to walk across the courtyard and relax on one of the wooden couches and meditate until the sun lifted over the horizon and he could celebrate the Shema prayer. He turned, studied the opposite side of the courtyard where the rooms were finished, and at the end of the eastern side of the wall, he saw a heap of something out of place.

The heap could be debris and waste waiting to be cleared away. Jacob didn't think so. Nothing had been placed on that side of the house in the last two or three days.

He stayed beside the wall, feeling the rough brick scrape across his right shoulder.

His heart pounded hard in his chest. Jacob felt the lift of awareness that always came just before a skirmish or battle. Any feeling or thought of tiredness or fatigue disappeared.

Jacob kept his right side close to the wall, glanced behind him. It was a habit left from leading his soldiers on night raids against the Babylonian army during the siege of Jerusalem

There was no-one behind him. He hadn't expected there to be. Only two of them remained alive.

The memory made him shiver. He pushed the thought aside, and moved slowly along the wall toward the pile.

Fifteen paces away, he felt the slick twist in his gut as he recognized the pile for what it was.

Jacob lowered the sword and changed direction toward the half-finished kitchen. He placed the sword on the top of the waist-high wall, picked up a sliver of kindling and uncovered the embers of the cooking fire. He blew carefully on the ashes until they glowed bright red in the darkness, then pushed the kindling in, holding it there until light flared.

Shielding the flame with his right hand, Jacob touched the kindling to the wick of a sesame oil lamp, held it there until the lamp caught.

The line of light on the eastern horizon was wider and brighter but Jacob still needed the lamp to see properly as he reached the pile.

What at first appeared to be rags was a ripped cloak bundled round a body. The legs were bound together, the left foot twisted at an impossible angle.

Jacob reached with his left hand for the shoulder of the cloak and rolled the body over. As the body shifted, the cloak flapped open revealing a naked torso with bruises and wounds across stomach, chest, and neck.

The man's face was a bloodied mask, his nose broken, eyes wide and looking at the sky without seeing.

Jacob felt the chill run up his spine. His throat closed up, and tears sprang into his eyes. He reached over, and very gently closed the man's eyes, saying a prayer as he did so.

Now there was one left alive.

Death at a Wedding

Jacob fought desperately to save Jerusalem from the Babylonian invaders. Injured and exiled, Jacob now builds a new life among his former enemies in the city of Babylon.

An unexpected death makes Jacob reassess everything he believes. Are his friends being truthful. Are the priests honest, or are darker forces at work in Babylon?

Pulling back the layers of lies and half-truths leads Jacob to a shocking last confrontation.

Get Death at a Wedding, the second Jacob and Miriam mystery at: https://books2read.com/DeathataWedding

The Corpse in the Courtyard

Jacob is devastated when he discovers the body of an old friend dumped at his home. The murder drags him into a conspiracy he's tried to avoid for many months. At odds with his own people, and the priests of the Babylonian temple, Jacob must rely on Miriam to determine truths and falsehoods from people neither of them trust.

It takes another violent death to point Jacob and Miriam in the right direction. A direction that threatens to cost Jacob his life, and condemn every Judean Exile into slavery.

Get The Corpse in the Courtyard, the third Jacob and Miriam mystery at: https://books2read.com/TheCorpseInTheCourtyard

Babylon Collections

Beginnings in Babylon

books2read.com/BeginningsInBabylon

Unexpected Companions

books2read.com/u/38yXvz

Making a New Start

books2read.com/NewStart

The Puzzle Store

Tales from the Puzzle Store

books2read.com/Puzzle

Christmas at the Puzzle Store

books2read.com/u/bxa7oe

Other Collections

Call Me Rhys

books2read.com/CallMeRhys

The Vatican Shadows

books2read.com/VaticanShadows

Mageweaver

books2read.com/Mageweaver

A Frailty of Heroes

books2read.com/Frailty

A Bag of Bodies

books2read.com/BagOfBodies

The Beach Bar on the Dune

https://books2read.com/u/3GJlod

From Ceres to Vesta

https://books2read.com/u/brEaeM

Where Infinity Begins

https://books2read.com/u/47091N